THE FOREIGNER

ARUN JOSHI

Orient
Paperbacks

DELHI | MUMBAI | HYDERABAD

ISBN: 978-81-222-0146-8

The Foreigner

Subject: Fiction

© Arun Joshi, 1993, 2010

New edition 2010
4th Printing 2014

Published by
Orient Paperbacks
(A Division of Vision Books Pvt. Ltd.)
5A/8, Ansari Road, New Delhi-110 002
www.orientpaperbacks.com

Cover design by Vision Studio

Printed at
Ravindra Printing Press, Delhi-110 006, India

Part One

1

*T*HEY UNCOVERED his face and I turned in spite of myself.
"Will you please look at the body, Mr. Oberoi?"

A dark bottomless hole gaped in place of the right eye. The sensual upper lip was gone, leaving behind a horrible grin that showed no sign of ending.

"Should I remove the sheet?"

"No," I said quickly. "Don't bother."

"Do you know him?"

"Yes. Babu Khemka. Babu Rao Khemka."

"Student?"

"Yes."

"Which department?" The man spoke tonelessly, his face without expression.

"Engineering," I said.

"Do you know where he lives?" the man asked. He took out a pack of Viceroys. The ad said Viceroy men were men of the world.

I was suddenly tired.

"No," I said, letting out a sigh in little jerks. "Somewhere on Pine Street." It was surprising that I had never been to Babu's place.

"Put him back," the man said to the attendant.

"What happened?" I asked because I thought it was expected of me.

"Car wreck on Mass Turnpike. Rolled off a bridge."

Tiredness crept up my legs, turning them to stone. My eyes felt overly dry and my throat contracted.

"May I leave?" I asked.

"Yes. Thanks for coming. The girl outside will give you some papers to sign."

I turned to leave.

"Do you know a girl named June Blyth?" the man asked.

"Yes," I said and waited for the worst.

He shrugged. "We found her picture in his wallet. Will you tell her?"

"Yes. I'll tell her," I said, relieved. After I signed the papers the girl asked if I wanted her to call a cab. I said I didn't know where I was going, so there was no point in getting a cab.

"Was he your friend?"

"Yes," I said, "and perhaps a bit more."

"I'm sorry," she said softly, and I thought that was what they all would tell me from now on.

It was rush hour and the Boston crowd milled around me. I stood on the pavement and tried to think. Nothing came to my mind except the rumble of engines and the screeching of tyres. Two girls with fancy parcels came by chewing gum. One of them said something to the other and they both laughed. I was sure they were laughing at me.

I turned around and peered at my reflection in the dirty window glass of a cheap clothing store. I did look strange. The whole thing had left me baffled. All along I had acted out of lust and greed and selfishness, and they had applauded my wisdom. When I had sought only detachment I had driven a man to his death. It all seemed very logical now that it had happened. A few hours before it would have seemed so improbable. You never expect death to hit somebody you know.

I realised I was counting the buttons on the cheap blue sport shirt in the window.

An old bald man with rimless glasses appeared from nowhere and asked if I would like to look at some shirts. I said I only wanted to make a phone call. He looked me up and down and said it would cost me a quarter. It was too high, but I wanted to talk to June without wasting any more time. As a matter of fact, I wanted to get the whole

8

business over with as soon as possible. I paid the man and dialled June's number. She said she would meet me at the cafe below.

When she walked through the revolving doors I began to see her in a new light. She carried death with her. She had been an accomplice in a murder and she didn't even know it. But ignorance of sin, like ignorance of the law, is no excuse. I ordered coffee for both of us. There was no point in asking what she wanted. It hardly mattered now.

June looked at my face searchingly. I avoided her eyes, so unnaturally full of fear and premonition.

"Babu is dead," I said after a while. There seemed to be no other way of saying it. I don't think she really believed it for a minute. I was right; she didn't realise we had killed a man. I hated myself, but for her I felt only pity.

"Babu is dead, June," I said again. "He had an accident on Mass Turnpike."

"Oh, God!" Her fingers trembled and she pressed them against her temples. In her distress she looked even more beautiful. "Oh, God," she said again, and then the tears came. I turned away because I couldn't stand to watch. I told her briefly what had happened. When I finished she said nothing. I sat and stared at the wall facing me.

Suddenly, the juke box burst upon the stillness of the little room, like the opening volley of a battle, and I started involuntarily. Ahead of me I could expect a long, long battle to forget the past. The waitress ambled leisurely by and asked if we wanted more coffee.

"No, thanks," I said. June had hardly touched her cup.

"Don't cry, June," I said when the waitress was gone.

"What am I to do, Sindi?"

I said it was too late to do anything.

Normally her crying would have torn me up. But my heart was already so full another drop or a hundred hardly mattered.

"I didn't want this to happen to him, Sindi."

"I know."

I wished I could have said the same thing for myself. I might not have willed it consciously, but in some foggy chamber of my being I must have waited for it to happen.

We finished our coffee and walked outside and stood under the ragged awning.

"Would you like to come to the hotel with me?" I asked.

"No, I would rather go back to work."

"Are you sure?"

June nodded, unable to speak, her eyes brimming with tears again.

"Goodbye then."

I turned to go and she lurched forward, clutching at my shoulders. She pressed her face against my chest and cried some more. My arms hung limp at my sides. I could feel her warm tears soak through my shirt.

"What shall I do, Sindi? What shall I do?"

My poor, poor girl, I thought. I rubbed her back to ease her crying. I said, "There is nothing you can do, my poor love. It is all over. I should have known better."

2

MANY MONTHS later, I was apprehensive as the Sikh taxi driver whizzed me through the dustladen streets of Delhi. Now and then he turned completely around in the seat, his face shining with sweat, and asked me for directions. I kept telling him I didn't know the place myself. I had never been to Mr. Khemka's house.

I would rather not have seen Mr. Khemka, but I thought it was expected of me since I was the one who had sent them the cable about Babu's death. Babu was a fool, but I had been sorry at the time of his death. Time had fossilized the tragic memory. I wondered how I was going to face these people who perhaps held him alive as a son and a brother. And what if they started crying or did something equally emotional? I tried to plan my reactions but I knew that was not possible. I had no idea what they were going to say. And what mask was I to put on if they knew? The thought made me uncomfortable and I wished again I hadn't come.

By some miracle the taxi driver had selected the right road and we were turning into Mr. Khemka's drive. It was too late to get out of it now.

The house was old and single-storeyed with a magnificent lawn that contrasted beautifully with the red gravel of the drive. Immense neem trees swayed gently in the midday breeze, dropping their ripe, yellow fruit in tropical profusion. A thick rubber hose lay snake-like across the garden, spouting water at random. The gardener, stripped to the waist, dozed in the shade, a hungry-looking child by his side.

I paid the taxi and walked towards the porch. I felt terribly hot in my tropical suit. My collar was soaked. I itched to loosen my necktie but dared not.

I passed through the porch and climbed the short steps into the spacious verandah where a couple of liveried servants chattered and polished glass. As I came upon them they fell silent and eyed me curiously. One of them asked what my business was. I said I had no particular business but I was Babu's friend.

The name was immediately effective and they showed me into a drawing room.

In everything I saw that day when I sat in Mr. Khemka's drawing room I looked for Babu's image. A huge portrait of him stared from the mantel. The photographer had touched it unnecessarily in a lot of places and Babu looked even more innocent than he had been in real life. And when a girl walked in and said she was Sheila, for a long moment I only searched for a resemblance between her and Babu.

"You must be Babu's sister," I said, getting up.

"I am. Won't you sit down?"

I sat down.

"Father will be in directly. What would you like to drink?"

I said I was thirsty and would like some water.

"Have a drink," she said.

I told her water was good enough.

She said she meant whisky or gin, or something like that.

I said I wouldn't mind having something like that after I had had some water.

A little dark man brought me a glass of water and I noticed how thin his wrists were. Babu had said the only poor people he knew were his servants.

"It must be very hot for you," Sheila said.

I said it must be hot for everybody, but their house was cool.

Then her father came in. For a moment I thought it was Babu,

11

grown suddenly old and risen from the dead. When Mr. Khemka shook my hand it gave me a clammy feeling.

"You are the one who sent the cable?" he asked.

"Yes, sir."

"When did you arrive?"

"Yesterday."

"Where are you staying?"

I gave him the name of the hotel.

"Good place. It belongs to a friend of mine."

"Have a drink," he said brusquely. I noticed a smile flicker across Sheila's lips.

I said I didn't mind.

I had a drink and for a while we chatted about the weather. Then he asked me, "When are you going home?"

"I have to look for a job first," I said, evading the question.

"Don't you want to see your family?"

I mumbled something to the effect that I didn't particularly care and hoped that Mr. Khemka would stop there. But he was not one to take no for an answer.

"Where do your parents live?"

I knew it would come sooner or later. It always did. I hated to talk about my parents. I hated the pity I got from people.

"I lost them when I was four," I said.

"Oh!" Both father and daughter looked uncomfortable.

"I am sorry," Mr. Khemka said finally. "How did it happen?"

For the hundredth time I related the story of those strangers whose only reality was a couple of wrinkled and cracked photographs.

I said they had been killed in an aircrash near Cairo and that I had been brought up by an uncle in Kenya. I wanted to add that I didn't particularly miss them, that it was too long ago for me to remember, but I thought that might be misconstrued.

There was a pause. A long pause. I looked at the empty glass in my hand and then at the richness of Mr. Khemka's drawing room. This was no doubt India's affluent society. Plush carpets, low streamlined divans, invisible lighting, bell buttons in every corner, and sculpture. That is where Babu must have played as a child. The rich Persian carpets, those sculpture-ridden walls must have concocted the innocence that destroyed him and very nearly buried me. Mr. Khemka and his daughter looked sympathetically at me as if they had come to my parents' funeral. I had the uncomfortable feeling that they were pitying me. I watched them and wondered if they knew the real story of Babu's death. Perhaps not, or they wouldn't have been so friendly.

We chit-chatted for another half hour. Mr. Khemka had been to New York and he thought Times Square wonderful. Sheila, of course, had her own views about America. She had never been there but she had apparently read quite a lot. Mr. Khemka had gone to America to sign a collaboration agreement for the manufacture of air-conditioners. He seemed proud of the deal that he had negotiated. He described some of the technicalities of the agreement which I could not grasp.

"Ours would be the first air-conditioner plant in the country," he explained elaborating unnecessarily. I said, "Babu told me you are already manufacturing quite a few electric appliances."

"Yes, we are." He noticed the empty glass in my hand and rang the bell for a servant. Then he went on to describe in some detail his different products. In between he pressed the bell several times. Since everything was lying just next to us I could have made the drink myself, but I hesitated, not knowing how it might be taken. Finally, when the servant appeared, Mr. Khemka lost his temper on him. Sheila, I noticed, was considerably embarrassed by his outburst.

Mr. Khemka continued to describe his business in detail. I let him talk. That suited me. After a while he returned to his American visit.

"After I came back, I decided to send Babu to America. I had thought it would make a man of him. And, of course, his training would have been of great help to us when he came back."

A lone fly, quite unexpected in that air-conditioned room, buzzed across the room and settled on my cheek.

"Of course," I said brushing the fly away.

"Were you long in America?" Mr. Khemka asked.

"About six years."

"And before that?"

"I was in London."

"Studying?"

"Yes," I said, a trifle tired.

"How long did you know Babu?" Sheila asked. She had spoken after a long while.

For just a fraction of a second I hesitated. "Almost the whole time he was there," I said.

The fly came back, reconnoitred, then dived suddenly and settled on my nose.

"He used to mention you frequently in his letters."

"Did he?" Then, for safety, I added. "We were good friends."

Somewhere a clock struck one. I put down my glass.

"Have another drink," Sheila said, moving towards the mobile trolley where a dozen bottles of imported liquor stood in a resplendent display. At the hotel they said foreign liquors could be had only in the black-market.

"No, thanks," I said. I stood up. "I must be going."

But Mr. Khemka would not hear of it. Why must I go, he asked, I must stay on for lunch. I had no reason to go, so I stayed on.

We lunched in an adjoining room, furnished as luxuriously and tastefully as the drawing room. We sat at the edge of an enormous rosewood dining table laid with expensive cut-glass and polished silver. Sheila sat at the head of the table. Behind her, in an alcove, stood a bronze figure of dancing Shiva. For a moment, just one brief moment, I was struck by the intense beauty of the divine dancer. America, India, Egypt, all mingled behind him in aeons of increasing rhythm. The dance went on unheeding, and yet comprehending all. What did it matter if Babu was dead, and I living merely to keep up appearances.

After lunch conversation centred around what I wanted to do in life. When I said I didn't know, Mr. Khemka frowned. He asked me what sort of job I was looking for.

"I want to do something meaningful," I replied, and then it occurred to me that the statement was a mistake.

"What do you mean by `meaningful'?" Mr. Khemka asked.

I wanted to say that it should be something that could make me forget myself, but I changed my mind.

I said, "Well, you know, something challenging and productive, something in my line, a production job, for example."

"What did you study?"

"Mechanical engineering."

"Did you like it?"

I cared two pins for all the mechanical engineers in the world, but I said "yes" because I wanted to end the conversation. I had not followed Mr. Khemka's line of thought and his next remark took me by surprise. "Well, I could give you a job in our factory," he said.

I searched his face. I didn't want a job given to me out of pity, or merely because he thought I was Babu's friend. But he looked businesslike.

"It is not a big job," he continued, carving out a little niche for me with his beautiful hands. "But I think you will like it, even though I must tell you it is more administrative than engineering in nature. You would be sort of a personal assistant to me, helping me in all my activities."

Now I sometimes wonder why I ever accepted his offer. Maybe I didn't care much what I did so long as I got away from myself. To refuse his offer would have meant many more days of painful brooding in silent hotel rooms. And then he talked so sweetly, so disarmingly, one could hardly refuse anything he asked.

Mr. Khemka's office was a cramped little place, much too small for his growing empire. It pleased him to refer to his business as a growing empire. During the first year I spent with him I came to realise that he really was a successful businessman. It was not until the growing empire crumbled that I understood how it was made to grow.

He had a plant near Delhi but the head office was in Delhi itself. It consisted of a large hall with three cabins at one end. In two of them Mr. Khemka and Sheila sat. The third built presumably for Babu, stood vacant. All the employees, including myself, sat in the hall in clean wooden rows where the pattern was changed every few weeks, depending upon Mr. Khemka's whims.

I was considered quite a misfit. My foreign background stood against me. Nobody hated me. I was too insignificant for that sort of thing. But I suspect they considered me a little too casual even though some of them envied me a bit for my light-heartedness.

What puzzled me from the beginning about Mr. Khemka's office was the mortal dread in which he and his daughter were held by the employees. The workers cringed before them as if the man and his daughter were malevolent spirits whose curse could be all-consuming. My life had carried me through strange places and I had seen men act from the ends of their tethers, but the servility I came across in Mr. Khemka's office was quite new to me.

I took a long time figuring out how I was expected to behave. I had no desire to cause a disturbance. Ultimately I decided to forget about the figuring. It would have been impossible for me to behave as the others.

With Mr. Khemka my relations were what might be called

15

cordial. I never took him seriously but was careful not to show it. He had the self-confidence of the wealthy. Even where I differed with him I did not make an issue of it. As a result we got along well. As a matter of fact after a period of initial trial he began to hand me fairly important assignments.

Being assistant to the Managing Director was being assistant to Mr. Khemka in everything. Besides helping him at the office I did a number of small chores. Attending the social parties at his house, for example, was one of my jobs.

I didn't quite know what was expected of me, at these parties but I tried to make myself as amiable as possible. It was all a bit of a hoax. Everybody knew it, but there was no point in talking about it. I suppose Mr. Khemka's guests knew what they were doing. Old men grown fat with success came with their plump wives. They drank and then they had gorgeous dinners. They talked of money and how to make more of it. They left the impression that they could buy up anybody they wanted. Perhaps they could, but it all sounded meaningless to me. I had read much of inequality in India; now I could see it masquerade as company law and the amendments of Parliament. I had no morals to apply one way or the other, but the fat men left me with a distinct feeling of being out of place. We were looking for two different worlds.

Occasionally, I ran into a lone beauty hidden away in this crowd of obesity. I would watch her chatting in a corner with some old nitwit and my heart would leap. Hypnotized, I would watch her dark liquid eyes flashing laughter, her small hands creating patterns of beauty with the tinkle of tiny bangles. I would watch the subtle swell of her golden belly showing beneath the gauzy sari and I would become aware of my own loneliness. Between her and me the chasm of a living world prevailed. I had a feeling that I was watching her from the edge of the world just where Death's kingdom began. But the feeling always passed.

Sometimes the ladies would ask me why I wasn't married and who my parents were, but by and large they ignored me. Later I was told that had I been richer and from a "respectable family" or had I belonged to a family at all, I would have had a much more difficult time avoiding offers of marriage.

In spite of all my handicaps I did have at least one person who keenly looked forward to my visits. It was Sheila. That girl had a passion, not for me, but her dead brother. Whenever I went to their house she cornered me on the edge of a sofa and asked me things about Babu. For some reason she never asked such questions at the office.

I liked her, but I tried to avoid questions as much I could. I didn't want to talk about Babu. To do so I would have had to talk about myself, and that would have been painful. I evaded her questions about Babu the best I could, but it was all a losing battle. Helplessly, I watched my past overtake me. I had travelled half the world to escape Babu's ghost and still it stalked me from behind those bronze statues. As Babu's friend, I had to talk. To have behaved in any other manner would have aroused needless suspicion. Over a period of six months, I told Sheila the beginning of our friendship but concealed its decay and hoped the curtain that covered the darkest of my existence would forever remain drawn.

3

IT WAS an unusally cold September evening when I first met Babu. I waited for him at Logan Airport in Boston. I had stood in the same spot waiting for the young adventurers every year for three years. I was hired by the foreign students' office to look after new Indian students. The office thought I liked the job; every year they sent me a note thanking me for my enthusiasm. In the beginning it had been interesting; it had made me feel important. Gradually it sank into routine, like opening envelopes or being a husband. But the worst of it lay in the emotional strain. Lonesome as they were these young innocents attached themselves to me. That, too, had fed my vanity in the beginning, but the strain of too many friendships had proved too much. I kept the job only because it added a few dollars to my meagre resources. Still, I almost hated myself as I waited for Babu and watched the spout of orange juice gushing behind the soda fountain in the lobby.

The public address system blared the arrival of the New York flight. Soon after, Babu entered the lobby twirling his hat self-consciously. Rounding a corner, he bumped into a young girl and apologised profusely. I caught his eye just as he left the girl. I introduced myself. He was taller and darker than I, and strikingly good looking. He wore a dark blue suit with enormous trouser cuffs. It enhanced his good looks, but the Indian stitching lent him a strictly non-Western appearance.

"How do you do, sir," he said, blushing.

"How are you? How was the flight?" I had all my questions ready. "It is somewhat cold here this evening," I added, varying my canned protocol.

"It was wonderful coming over the Alps and then the Atlantic. The hostess was very nice. And London was so beautiful and all. I just wanted to stay on there. One of my uncles is studying there, you know."

Babu prattled on as we drove back to the city. His uncle was studying medicine in London and was supposed to be clever with women. I thought of June. I had to see her after dropping Babu at the Y.M.C.A. Babu kept leaning out of the window to gaze at the more gorgeous pieces of American affluence.

"America is just, just much more splendid than what I had ever imagined," he exclaimed. For a moment I thought I almost liked him. I had experienced the same sensations when I first walked around New York.

Old men in the Y.M.C.A. lounge smiled at us warmly as we went up. That is where they spent their evenings, waiting for death. The room was stuffy and smelled of deodorant. I kept myself busy opening windows and turning on the radiator. I knew Babu was baffled and wanted to talk. They always clung to whoever offered them a hand in those early days. But I didn't have a strong arm that I could lend to Babu. I had my own problems.

I got away from him as soon as I could, promising to meet him the next evening. I walked down the stairs wishing God had given me greater strength for enduring the burdens of friendship.

From across the lounge an old man shouted at me, "How's your asthma, son?" It was the pharmacist from the college infirmary.

"Bad, Mr. Clark," I shouted back, "Bad."

"You think you'll live?"

"One hopes for the best."

Mr. Clark broke into thunderous, lonely laughter as if that was the funniest joke he had heard all day.

I thought of June, of her warm body beside me in the growing dark and a good hot meal afterwards. She would be waiting for me.

The next day the weather turned. The sun had shone all day and it had grown warm. The twilight was clear and it seemed to linger a long time amidst the spires and domes of Boston, its peaceful texture broken only by the periodic vulgarity of neon lights. My asthama was dormant. I was glad to be alive.

At our second meeting I sensed something eerie about Babu. I didn't realise it then, but later I discovered what it was. His eyes gathered a peculiar haunted look whenever he was depressed. I came to know that look well in the months we were together. It was the first thing I looked for when they called me to identify his body.

His eyes were clouded now as we stood in the narrow room. He said he was fed up with the place. It gave him a creepy feeling to see all those old men around. He wanted to get out and go somewhere. He said he wanted some fresh air.

I asked if he had been in all day.

"More or less. I went out in the morning to the registrar's office and then to the foreign students' advisor. I tried to talk to some of the people on the street but they are so damn uninterested. The moment they find out you have nothing particular in mind they excuse themselves and get away."

"Americans are a busy people, you know," I said.

"But one would expect them to show some interest in foreigners."

I asked why. I was just curious.

"Well, just because they are foreigners! If we meet any Americans in Delhi we take great interest in them, don't we?"

"I don't know," I said. "I have never been to Delhi."

"No?" Babu's eyebrows went up. "But you are an Indian, are you not?"

I said I was from Kenya and he looked disappointed.

"Where did you study?" he asked.

"East Africa and London." I perched on the edge of the bed and looked at the rug. "Look here, Babu," I said. "Don't take these things to heart. You are in for a few surprises, but Americans are a pretty good people on the whole. You'll soon find friends of your sort."

I didn't believe all that, but I thought it would do Babu some good.

19

"Anyway," he shrugged, "I'm glad you are here. Let us go out somewhere."

We drove down to the Harvard campus and then to the river. The low sun cut a shimmering triangle of gold in the blue water. It reminded Babu of home. They had three houses in Delhi and a villa in Mussoorie. "Mussoorie would be beautiful these days. Sheila must be going skating every day. And in the evening they would all sit in the verandah watching the sunset." Tears of homesickness glistened in his eyes.

I stopped the car at a small park on the edge of the river and we sat gazing out across the water at the sail boats. I had never seen Mussoorie but I imagined it would be like many other unending mountain landscapes. Valley after valley, submerged first in gold and then in darkness. Grey smoke curling up from dwarf houses far down the mountain side. I had never had a home but I could see with Babu's eyes and I could feel the loneliness welling up slowly in his breast.

Cars dashed by carrying baggage and weekend revellers. Babu stared at passing young girls and desire was in his eyes.

"Do you know many girls?" he asked me.

"No," I said.

"But you must? You are so charming."

"While you are in America, Babu, don't fall in love. It does nobody any good. Let's go and eat somewhere."

I don't know why I said it but at the time it came out almost naturally. Perhaps I wanted him to be happy and keep away from mistakes which many others made.

Babu looked puzzled and I wondered if I had conveyed anything. Perhaps not, but I didn't feel like pressing the point. That would have involved me unnecessarily.

We had dinner at a drive-in. I tried to discuss his plan of studies with him but Babu never stopped talking of home and girls. His father, he said, was very strict. He would be very angry if he found out that his son was running around with strange women.

"But you are not running around with strange women," I said.

"Not yet, but who knows?" Babu smiled mysteriously, as if he had a number of clandestine meetings already lined up. "What is the good of coming to America if one is not to play around with girls?" he asked.

20

"Of course, I don't want to marry anyone. I just want to gain experience, you know." He smiled. It was a mischievous smile, reflecting some secret image of an Indian Casanova.

I heard him with a mixture of premonition and boredom. That was how they all began when they came. They wanted to play around. They forgot that one couldn't play around without playing with oneself and that could be fatal.

4

I MET June at one of those balls the International Students Association laid out every year. I first saw her back. I was sitting against the bar facing the dance floor. She was dancing with a Formosan who was in my advanced physics class. She wore a blue dress. It was one of those creations that make women sort of ethereal. There was a deep cut at the back and I could see the soft smooth muscles of her shoulders. That is what Kathy had looked like from a distance. They were the same height. But what reminded me most of Kathy was June's hair. It was a mass of gold, bordering on red. Because of the resemblance I couldn't take my eyes off her. I followed her back across the floor. And then I found myself wishing that she would turn so I could see her face. But she never turned and I lost track of her.

I went back to my drinking. I had to stick around that place until the party was over. I was supposed to be one of the ex-officio hosts. Like all balls, the whole thing was quite a fraud. It was intended to bring foreigners in contact with Americans, but all it ever achieved was animosity; everybody ended up hating the Americans all the more. I don't know why it happened. It was not that the Americans showed off or misbehaved or anything. As a matter of fact they all were very courteous. Yet, something about it—a feeling that it was a bit of a charity or something—rubbed people the wrong way. It is one thing to be invited to somebody's house for a party, quite another to go to a public hall, buy a ticket and then search the place for a girl you can dance with. I hated it. I never went to those things except as an ex-officio host.

I drank and watched the crowd bob up and down in the huge mirror behind the bar. All those faces distorted in the cheap mirror made me feel even more like an alien. Except for the bartender and me there wasn't a soul in the room who wasn't dancing or talking or beating his feet to the music. It is remarkable how you can be in a crowded room like that and still feel lonely, like you were sitting in your own tomb.

One of the blobs dissociated from the mob and started getting bigger until I recognized it as the girl whose back I had been watching. She came and sat down near me and asked for a coke. As a rule I never stare at people. But I couldn't take my eyes off this one. It wasn't that she was extremely pretty or sophisticated or anything. She had those large blue eyes that shone like marbles and a sweet little mouth. And she had a way of shaking her locks that made me want to touch them. She turned and caught me looking at her.

She smiled at me. "Where are you from?"

That just about spoiled everything. I wished she hadn't asked that question. Everybody always asked the same silly question. "Where are you from?" as if it really mattered a great deal where I was from.

"I am from Kenya."

"That's in Africa, isn't it?"

I nodded. I was still immersed in those large wondering eyes. Then she said something that took me by surprise.

"Why do you look so sad?" she asked.

I snorted, but her face remained serious. So I just kept quiet.

"Why aren't you dancing?"

I said I didn't like dancing and furthermore I didn't know it too well. She slid from her stool and took my hand.

"Come on, I'll teach you."

I didn't want to dance. Why was I walking out on the floor? She was being good to me and I didn't have the heart to refuse. Luckily the band was playing a fox-trot. That was the only step I knew.

She didn't look at me while we danced except when I took a wrong turn and stepped on her feet or something. Then she threw back her head, looked straight into my eyes and loosened a ripple of laughter.

22

The crowd pressed us together and I could feel the softness of her limbs. Her palm was warm against my neck. Beneath my fingers I could feel the suppleness of her waist. And then I began to want her—not sexually, but just to remain there dancing with her after everybody went home. But I knew it wasn't possible and I didn't feel particularly let down when she said she had to leave. I would have liked to take her home just to be with her for a while longer. But what was the point?

I went back to my seat at the bar. My drink was still there and so were the grotesque faces in the mirror. There was something strange about the girl. She had affected me in an unusual way. I put my hand to my face, trying to capture the little vapour of perfume that still seemed to come from somewhere. And then it struck me that she was the first woman I had held for almost two years.

I wished I could talk to somebody. They had changed the bartender and I had nothing to say to the new one. He gazed at me from time to time with the faked lack of interest that bartenders always try to affect. He filled my glass quickly when I drained it.

Finally he said, "Why don't ya' go dance, fella?"

I said I didn't feel like it and, besides, I didn't know anybody.

"There's plenty a' girls around. Why don't ya' get hold a' one?"

I didn't know what to say, so I just grinned.

"If you are bored, why don't ya' go home?" he asked. I guessed he, too, just wanted to talk to somebody.

"I can't", I said. "I'm the host."

"How come ya' don't know nobody?"

I told him I was an ex-officio host. He nodded and moved away to wash some glasses. He probably didn't know what an ex-officio host was.

I looked at my watch. It was eleven-thirty. The hall closed at midnight. They would soon start leaving so they could have a few minutes of necking in the cars before the girls' dorms closed. There was nothing for me to do but wait until they cleared out.

Gradually they started to leave. Strangers parted on the doorstep promising to meet again, knowing full well they didn't mean it. It was the American way. There was a big rush at the bar just before closing time. Latin-American boys in red jackets yelled at each other in Spanish as they pushed their money forward. Their dates pulled daintily at filtered cigarettes. "One for the road,' they all said. All that money for the road. If only I could get hold of some of that money, I wouldn't be sitting there supervising their silly revelries.

After the place emptied I strode around the hall. The bartender had disappeared suddenly. He'd said he had a date. What a time to have a date!

In the rush I'd forgotten the girl. But now the memory came back with painful sweetness. Halfway through my money counting I got up and went to the spot where I held her last. I raised my hands to my face and tried to inhale her fragrance; but it was gone. My fingers smelled only of old coins and sweaty greenbacks. I went back to my counting.

I thought about her on the way home, and just before I went to sleep I saw her float right up against the window. I couldn't resurrect her in detail but I saw the mass of golden hair, the blue eyes and the pink lips. And I had to admit to myself that I was a lonely man.

For some days after that I thought of June occasionally. Once or twice, as I lay awake in my bed, her face would materialise in the darkness. Her blue dress stood out against the white cupboard, her hair almost brushing against my cheek. I wanted to meet her again but nobody seemed to know her. I once told Karl, my roommate, about her. He was thoughtful about it, but he didn't understand. Nobody saw her as I did. As the days went by, the memory wore thinner until I could no longer recall her face. The memory would have died altogether; but after a few months I saw her again.

Every year, just before the spring term started, the Foreign Students Office gave a beer party for foreign students on the sand banks near the river. One bought a ticket for two dollars that entitled one to drink all the beer he wanted. These were tiresome affairs and I attended only because I was one of the hosts.

Karl sang loudly as we drove to the place. Singing was a habit when he was behind the wheel. He was Austrian, but to all appearances he seemed to have abandoned his homeland. He and I had approached our landlady at the same time for the flat. Rather than force her to choose between us, we decided to share it. That was the beginning of our friendship.

Karl wound up the song suddenly and I asked what it was about. "It was about a girl."

"I could have guessed as much. Do you miss Austria sometimes?"

"Yes, sometimes. But not much."

"Why did you leave in the first place?"

He was silent for a while, then he said, "There were a number of things. I was always hungry, for one thing. It was terrible after the war. Then I hated the way my stepmother brought lovers home after my father died. And one day when she got drunk and tried to seduce me, I left."

I examined his handsome profile. His eyes had narrowed and the grey sky lit them with a peculiar intensity. Girls who held that beautiful head didn't know the wounds they kissed.

"They already have the fire going," Karl said. He steered the car carefully onto the bumpy road leading to the picnic spot. A moth-like glow spread gently out of the woods a half mile away.

The crowd was larger than the ones in previous years. The dean had proudly said the university was attracting more foreign students every year. They were noisy. Karl and I sat on the edge of the crowd and drank our first beer. There was very little else to do. The fire was good but the grass felt cold and wet. I wondered if it would give me asthma.

I peered closely at the dimly lit faces. They all seemed new. Only the new ones came to these parties. I wondered what the old ones did for celebrating the arrival of spring. Perhaps they had found new friends. Or may be they didn't mark the changing seasons. Each season was the same: working late into the night, eating alone in cheap cafeterias, attending weekend cooking sessions at the flat of a countryman. This was the sum total of a foreign student's existence.

"Quite an international crowd," I said to Karl.

"Quite an international crowd," Karl repeated.

"You sound bitter," I laughed.

"I am not bitter. I am just fed up."

"Fed up with what?"

"Fed up with many things. Fed up with the way we pretend to have forgotten the past and yet all the time we are looking for an opportunity to revive it. Fed up with puerile demonstrations of love. Fed up with my own self-importance."

"What would you like to do?"

25

"I don't know." Karl said. "That's the whole trouble. I don't know what I should do. Most of the time I try not to think of it. Actually, it is only when I am with you that I even think about it."

Karl got started on what was wrong with the world, with America and Europe and Asia. I listened for a while, grunting occasionally to let him know I was listening. But after a time I even stopped grunting and lost track of what he was saying. My own mind drifted, and when it came back Karl was talking about war and atomic weapons. He waved his hand towards the gay crowd.

"Out of this bunch you will get your future atomic wizards, your missile boys, and yet there they sit, pretending to be innocent of their menace, caressing women whose kids they will blow up some day."

I said it was likely. But I didn't see what he or I could do about it. I wasn't interested. What was the point in talking about it?

Karl sensed my lack of interest and got up and staggered away to the beer stand. Halfway there, two girls caught hold of him and pulled him down. Karl was young and beautiful as a Greek god.

So what about the world? I was born an Indian and had been spat upon; had I been a European, I would have done the spitting. What difference did it make? I would still die and be forgotten by the world. And spitting hadn't made the world's big shots any happier than we were. What was the point, then, in fighting these straw men who suffered as much at the hand of existence as I? Below me in the dark I could hear the river's quiet song. Its rush would outlast me, carrying on its subtle music long after this crowd was put to the grave.

Suddenly my head came down in a violent sneeze and my lungs hurt. My eyes got bleary with tears. It looked like I was going to have another attack of asthma. I wanted to talk with someone about it. I wondered if the pain that was entirely my own would make sense to anybody else.

Maybe the fire would help. I stood up and pressed into the crowd. It closed behind me like the sea around Pharaoh's legions. As I moved, the language changed until each layer seemed to have its own tongue. It was like switching a radio from one alien wave length to another. Here and there I picked up a word in French or a phrase in Spanish but they didn't convey much; I had ceased being curious about other people's conversation.

I sat down near the fire. Karl was there with a girl. He was drunk. Someone picked up a guitar and strummed a gay Mexican tune and then a whole sector of the circle broke into song, clapping the beat. The clapping spread to those who didn't even understand the song. Unlike pain, happiness can be shared. It is aloneness in suffering that makes men selfish.

The fire was dying and the evening breeze was chilly. I sneezed again. Not once, but a dozen times. Water flowed from my eyes. I could have been crying at the thought of the impending misery.

From the other side of the fire Karl watched me intently, his head on the broad lap of his girl friend. I got up and walked towards the parking lot.

"Sindi, are you ill?" Karl called. He had stood up a little unsteadily abandoning his luxurious pillow. He knew I had attacks of asthma.

"Yes, I'm going home."

"Come, I will take you."

"No, Karl. You stay. The party has just begun. I can easily find a ride back to town. Plenty of people will be going that way."

Karl insisted for a while but when he found me stubborn he turned away swearing.

I stood in the graveyard of cars waiting for an angel. I knew very few people would be returning so early. But I didn't want to spoil Karl's evening.

Suddenly, one of the monsters sprang to life very near me. The car backed onto the dirt road, roared ahead, then almost knocked me down when it jolted to a stop where I stood in the blinding light.

"Could you give me a ride into the city?" I asked.

"Sure!" It was a girl. If I had known I wouldn't have stopped the car. But it was too late to back out now.

"Haven't I seen you before?" the girl asked. We lurched forward, sending stones right and left.

I looked at her. The blonde hair fluttered in the air. "My God." I whispered, "it is you." And then I was ashamed of having shown so much excitement.

"My name is June. June Blyth."

Out on the highway the car picked up speed. Self-consciously I watched the white dividing line unwind before us like a gigantic tape. I had almost forgotten her, had been so excited about her and now that I was face to face with her again I had nothing to say.

"How did you like the party?" she asked.

"It was all right."

"Going home rather early, aren't you?"

In all the excitement I had forgotten I was ill. Her remark brought back my illness with cruel reality. My nose was by now completely blocked. I could feel a storm rising at the bottom of my lungs and tried to choke it off. Gradually it enveloped my entire body. Panic wrung the last ounce of self-control out of me. Suddenly I broke into a violent fit of coughing and sneezing. I wanted to spit out of the window but thought June would be disgusted, so I spat into a handkerchief instead. I knew she was staring at me. I tried not to care, but I couldn't help feeling self-conscious. When I finished coughing I turned towards her.

"Are you ill? she asked.

"Yes. Nothing very serious."

She had slowed the car to a crawl a few minutes before. Now she brought it to a stop.

"Can I help?"

"No, I'll be all right." There was nothing she could do anyway.

"Would you like to go for a drive in the country? Maybe the air would do you some good."

I knew it would make me worse, but even with that, I wanted to prolong the ride back with her. I said I didn't care either way, but I would go with her if she felt like it. "Where are we going?"

"There is a nice country road on the left further down the road. I just love driving there at night."

The woods grew thicker as we went deeper. It was almost as if we had known each other for years. A rabbit suddenly darted from one side. For a split second it paused in the middle of the road, confused and blinded by the headlights, then darted off to the other side. The road was unpaved and wet after the rains. Puddles of water shone like liquid silver. The car skidded dangerously at times as we barrelled through the night.

I am not very good at remembering events, but for some reason I always remember the beginning and end of an affair. Even now that evening with June comes to my mind and I can't help wondering at the quickness with which we began to like each other. But the thought worried me as we slid along the muddy road. I really didn't want to start another affair. And yet I did not want to lose her again after she had dropped me home.

"Where do you live?" I asker her.

She told me. I had not heard of the street before but I made a mental note of it.

"You attend all these foreign students' get-to-gethers, do you?" I asked.

"Yes, most of them, anyway."

"I suppose you like them."

"Yes. By and large. I like meeting people from different countries, especially people from Asia. They are so much gentler—and deeper—than others, don't you think?"

I said I didn't know. I hadn't found them any different.

It must have been a half hour or so later when we reached some sort of a clearing. It was a wide open space fringed by tall poplars. The moon was full. The ground was purple and blue, the kind of blue that stone acquires in moonlight. Another car was parked at the far end. Lovers.

"This is Devil's Playground. What's your name?"

"Sindi," I said.

"Are you all right now, Sindi?"

I said I was feeling better. But I knew the worst was yet to come.

"Do you get these attacks often?"

"No, not very often. Three or four times a year."

"It must be painful."

"Yes. But it is good to be reminded once in a while how miserable one is."

June chuckled quietly. "I told you you are a queer person."

Then she turned serious.

She looked at me for a long time, thinking.

"Do you believe in God?'

I was surprised at her question.

"Why do you ask that?"

"There is something strange about you, you know. Something distant. I'd guess that when people are with you they don't feel like they're with a human being. Maybe it's an Indian characteristic, but I have a feeling you'd be a foreigner anywhere."

She said it so matter-of-factly that we might have been discussing the weather. She had not taken her eyes off me for a single moment. I looked about myself uncomfortably. Talking about myself always makes me ill at ease.

The lovers in the other car clung to each other on the rear seat. I wondered if there was anything more human and less foreign about them, or her, or the rabbit we had nearly killed on the road. But I said nothing. I didn't want to get into an argument.

She asked me again if I believed in God. I said I didn't know, but I supposed I didn't.

"I thought every Hindu believed in God."

"They ought to," I said, "But some of them get mixed up about it."

She giggled, and that surprised me because I had been trying to be serious. I thought it was a true statement of things.

"Anyway I can't really be called a Hindu. My mother was English and my father, I am told, a sceptic. That doesn't seem like a good beginning for a Hindu, does it?"

June giggled again.

"But you do seem to be at peace with yourself."

She surprised me again.

"Why do you say that?"

"Oh, I don't know. That was the first feeling I had when I saw you at the dance the other day. There you were, sitting hunched over your drink, expressionless, watching the world."

"We all have our masks, you know."

A little later I said, "What about you? Do you believe in God?"

"I used to. I was born a Catholic and I was a great churchgoer until I was fifteen."

"And then?"

"Then something happened. One Sunday everything seemed false, the opposite of what it had been. Everybody around me seemed to be play-acting. The priest read his sermons just like my uncle read the markets aloud from the newspaper every morning." She paused for a while, thinking, and then raised her hands, palm upwards, in front of her, eyes growing larger. "I don't know what happened really."

I was embarrassed by her personal talk. To change the subject I asked her where she worked. She gave me the name of an insurance company in Boston where she worked as a statistician.

30

"That is all I know," she said modestly pushing a golden lock of hair away from her cheek.

Her profession hardly seemed to fit in with her personality, but I made no comment.

She fell silent, too. Another bout of sneezing started. I knew I should go home. But I didn't want to leave. Was that the beginning of another affair? It needn't be, I told myself. But I couldn't hide from myself the fact that I wanted her.

"Shall we go back?" I suggested finally. "I think my asthma is going to get worse."

"Why don't you take some medicine? Haven't you got any?"

That reminded me. I had a couple of capsules in my jacket pocket I'd forgotten about. I fished one out and swallowed it.

June backed the car around, the headlights probing far into the woods. The lovers looked up and then went back to their business.

The car bumped along the road, skidding now and then in the mud. A few yards ahead of us a large wet patch of road shone like a pit full of mercury.

"Watch that!" I said. "Looks like deep mud."

"Don't worry, it's nothing," June smiled.

The car fell a few inches when we entered the bright patch. I saw June straining at the wheel, trying to keep the car on the road. Then we came to a stop. The wheels still whirled.

"We're stuck," June said.

"Try the reverse."

She shifted gears and the car moved backward a few inches, then the tyres lost grip again.

"It's no use," June said.

We got out and looked at the wheels. They were in mud up to the hub caps. There was no hope of getting out without help. The air smelled of burnt rubber. We looked at each other, at the trees and the sky. All was quiet except for our breathing and the eerie sound of dew dripping from the trees.

"Never expose yourself to dew," the doctor had told me. I strained to hear my breathing and I thought of a gust of wind howling through a subterranean lagoon. I was afraid and worried.

"How far is the nearest farm house?"

"About five miles."

"Well, what do we do?"

31

"I don't know," she said. "Wait, I guess, until somebody comes along."

Suddenly I was angry with her. I had told her to be careful of the patch and yet she had landed right into the muck. And now I was going to gasp for breath right in front of her. My anger made me even more miserable.

We sat in the car and waited. June switched on the radio. Some kind of syrupy jazz flowed out like glue. It swung up and down soft and lusty. June switched it off when I said I didn't like it. We were silent for several minutes. My breathing was getting noticeably difficult. June asked how long I had had asthma.

"As long as I can remember. They say my mother had it."

"How do you know it's not some sort of mental disorder," June asked, "I mean some sort of a psychosomatic problem?"

"I knew you'd get around to that," I retorted, irritated. "You Americans! Every illness in a mental disorder like every song is rock'n roll. Yesterday I went to the doctor for some medicine and he said I needed a girl."

"Maybe you do."

"Maybe."

"Now really don't you want a girl?"

I sighed tiredly. This was going to be a regular psycho-analysis session. It would have been funny, normally, but crouched there with my lungs filling up it could only be tiresome. Didn't I want a girl? I guess everybody wanted a girl for some reason or another. Only some of us thought the price was too heavy for the luxury. Terms of love are often usurious. Didn't I want a girl? Next she would ask me what I thought of American girls. And that is just what she did.

I said I didn't know any but I imagined they should be all right except that they behaved so much like boys. This set her laughing again.

"Why do you think so?"

I said I couldn't pinpoint it but that was the total impression most foreigners got. American girls did their hair like boys, they dressed like boys and they bullied you around.

"What about Indian girls? Don't they have any faults?" June was beginning to get a little hot under the collar.

A blast of cold air caught my chest and I broke into a fit of coughing. It grew violent. The more I tried to suppress it, the more persistent it became. My lungs were bursting and I couldn't stop it. It had come I thought. It had come at last. Soon I would be gasping for air, turning purple, and June would be watching. I felt ashamed and humiliated. Then it stopped and left my chest, heaving like a pair of bellows. I leaned over and rested my head on the dashboard. My shoulders hunched in the characteristic pose of all asthmatics. My eyes were closed and tears poured from them.

"Are you feeling very bad?" June asked. She made no attempt to hide her anxiety.

"Yes."

"Can I help?"

"No, I don't want any help."

For a moment all was silent except for the sound of my wheezing breath and dew dripping from the leaves outside. Then I heard June move. Before I knew what was happening her hand was unbuttoning my shirt, then moving inside, gently massaging my chest to ease, my breathing. I was surprised and then I felt things cracking up inside me. One after another my defences fell apart and I realised how foolish I was. Vain and foolish like a peacock. I turned my face towards her and suddenly was overcome with an almost unbearable wave of self-pity. Illness and physical pain had drained my will and I felt like crying.

"My poor, poor, boy," she murmured.

Then she slid away and pulled me down in the seat with my head resting in her lap. She caressed my chest and her long fingers played tenderly with my hair. My breath was coming more easily, but the coughing had left me exhausted. Just before I went to sleep I wondered what had soothed me—the capsules or June.

An asthmatic's sleep is full of bad dreams. In this one I was on a ship with another passenger whose face I couldn't see. We were heading for a beach at an unbelievable speed. I was sure they would change course, before it was too late. But they didn't. The prow hit the beach and I could hear the propellers gnaw at the sand. I tried to walk off but my hands were glued to the rail. I looked pleadingly at the other passenger. To my relief, I discovered it was June. But she only sighed and walked past me off the ship. Then everything was weirdly bright as if bonfires burnt behind my eyes. I tried frantically to free my hands. Then I woke up.

June was not in the car. I sat up. She was talking to some people outside. Slightly to the right a car was parked in front of us. It was the car we had seen in the clearing. The girl jumped about like a monkey giggling and laughing, encouraging the boy as he stood ankle deep in mud trying to tie a rope between the cars. June stood at one end holding up her skirt, ostensibly trying to help the boy with a torch. But more often her torch was directed at me. Now and then she mocked the poor boy and everybody laughed.

Everything was in a different light now. It was all a big joke. When the car was out and the lovers gone, we laughed. June put her arms around my neck.

"And how is the sick boy now?"

In the dim light she seemed strange and beautiful. I was full of love and sadness at the same time. Even if I loved her and she loved me it would mean nothing, nothing that one could depend upon. I was not the kind of man one could love; I had learnt that long ago. For June it took almost a year to find out.

Part Two

5

*I*T WAS the day the monsoon broke when the income tax man came for the first time to Mr. Khemka's office. I remember this because I couldn't tear myself away from the dark rumbling sky and I resented his intrusion.

"I'm from the income tax office," he said for the third time.

"Yes? What can I do for you?"

"We sent you a number of communications regarding certain matters. You have not bothered to reply them," he said with a sneer.

"No? I am sorry. But you see I don't think I am the man you want to see. Serious problems like income tax are handled by the boss, Mr. Khemka himself." He fixed me with a suspicious eye, so I added, "I just work here."

"I might say that I am not here to cut jokes."

"I'm sorry. Have you seen Mr. Khemka?"

"No. I have made enquiries, and I want them answered. And I am here only because this happens to be our Courtesy Week. Otherwise, I would have summarily summoned you to my office."

I liked that phrase, summarily summoned. It was musical.

"Just one of those fads of some fat minister," he bawled in a sudden burst of anger. "Election stunt, this courtesy stuff, if you ask me! All year we kick people's bottoms and then we give them a week of courtesy. Mind you, I am not saying that they don't deserve the kicking, but still I would rather kick them all year than make a fool of them with this courtesy stuff."

37

"You sound like an honest man. Mr...."

"What do you mean?" He sat up in his chair. And then I pitied his plump figure wedged tightly into the narrow chair. He might have been born sitting in it.

"Nothing," I said resignedly, "I meant nothing."

The income tax man leaned forward and planted his palms on the table. Drops of perspiration stood on his forehead, and behind the thick lenses of his spectacles his eyes were strangely wild. His voice rose above the monotonous grind of the overhead fan.

"I wouldn't talk of honesty, Mr. Oberoi, if I were you." It was a suggestion, a tense mysterious whisper meant to convey a great wrong. He paused to search my face for a reaction.

I didn't know what he expected of me or why he had picked on me for his cryptic remarks. He seemed a bit of a maniac to me, but then, ever since I had come to India many people had seemed maniacs to me. They all took themselves so seriously. I looked longingly out of the window at the dark clouds and wished he would leave. But he was on a high horse, rattling a sabre.

"Don't pretend that the rich people are the only honest people in the world," the income tax man said darkly. "I know a thing or two about them. If I were the minister this whole office would be wound up and handed over to the proletariat!"

"Proletariat?" I said slightly puzzled. "What has the proletariat to do with this business here. Anyhow, aren't most of us working here proletarian?"

"You are petty bourgeois." The way he said it, I half expected him to spit in my face. He took a deep breath and sat very straight in his chair.

"India is working towards a new age. Mr. Oberoi," he said grandly. "An age in which each man will be equal to another."

"Of course," I said politely.

"It is only people like you and Mr. Khemka who are holding back the revolution."

That man had a tremendous capacity for provoking people. I slid into the argument in spite of myself.

"The revolution may come." I said. "And you know what will happen when it does. You will be shot. I will be shot. Muthu there will probably be shot. The rest will remain unchanged. The charlatans you wish to destroy will just turn around and put on another mask."

"A few individuals don't matter. What is important is that the proletariat will rule."

"The proletariat you speak of will most likely be corralled into communes and driven like slaves."

"That may be in the beginning," said the income tax man. "Sacrifice is inevitable in a revolution."

"That is precisely where you're wrong. There is never a beginning. Nor is there an end. There is no end to suffering, no end to the struggle between good and evil."

There was not much use in talking. Neither his presence nor his arguments made sense to me. He continued to talk excitedly about Capitalism and Socialism and tyranny of the rich but I paid no heed.

Then he asked me how long I had been working for Mr. Khemka. I told him about five months. He leaned over the desk and whispered urgently, "You should get out. You don't belong here."

It had never struck me that one had to belong. Faintly, deep within me, a little brazen alarm bell began ringing. I began to wonder how serious Mr. Khemka's income tax problems really were. But what difference did it make? I was not involved.

"I worked here myself," he continued, pressing close to my face. "This place is *vicious*!"

"I don't know what you mean Mr...." As far as I was concerned, every place was equally vicious.

"My name is Mr. Ghosh."

Muthu, my assistant, had been listening. Now he came along with a couple of glasses of lime juice. He thrust one of the glasses into my right hand and at the same time slipped a crumpled ball of paper into my left. Mr. Ghosh quaffed his juice in two or three gulps, then wiped his mouth and brow with a tattered handkerchief.

I smoothed the strip of paper on my knee behind the desk. "It'll be advisable for Ghosh to see Miss Khemka." Everything was merely advisable in Muthu's language; nothing was ever definite. He understood the ultimate futility of human effort.

I turned to Mr. Ghosh. "About your errand, I'm afraid I don't know anything about it, but it would certainly be advisable for you to visit Miss Khemka. She is Mr. Khemka's daughter, you know." I stood up and gestured towards her office, without giving him another chance to get distracted. "She is in now."

Sheila was reading a novel which she quickly put aside when we went in. I thought a shadow passed over her face when I told her Mr. Ghosh's errand.

Yes, the communications had been received. No, she couldn't reply to them. The various implications still had to be studied.

I knew I was not wanted in the room. When I returned to my desk, Muthu told me Ghosh was quite a menace. He might have been for all I knew. Anyway, he had nothing to do with me and as such I couldn't care less whether he was a menace or not.

"He used to work here," Muthu explained.

"So I gathered. He doesn't seem to have enjoyed it very much."

"No. I am afraid things did become a little unpleasant towards the end."

"What happened?"

"I don't know the details. Some personal feud between Mr. Khemka and Ghosh. You see, Ghosh is quite a bitter man. He claims to be a revolutionary and all that. He had organized a clerical union here. Mr. Khemka and he did not get along."

The sky had begun to clear. In the west the sun suddenly broke through. In the slums across the street, bundles of soggy humanity shuffled out of their huts and spread their miserable rags to dry. Full-breasted women, their thighs naked under wet saris, scurried back and forth like animals quarrelling over small bits of tin. Naked children rolled in the filthy pools, squealing with delight. These were the people to whom Ghosh would hand over our office. I didn't mind. But what good would it do them? What they needed were cheap prophylactics so they could copulate with greater freedom. Anyway, that was what I would have desired if I had been fortunate enough to have been born with their simpleness of mind. But I knew they couldn't get their prophylactics without inheriting the chaos of my being. I knew that in thousands of offices the abominable wheel of industrialization was grinding on inevitably. And we who pretended to be the masters were driven before it like bits of paper on a windy day.

Bright red buses of the Delhi Transport Undertaking sloshed through the mud splattering pedestrians with grime. In spite of the rain they were full; in India things are always full whatever the circumstances. A horde of hawkers had appeared from nowhere making a brisk sale of rotting fruit and gluey sweetmeats that passed well with slum-dwellers.

Muthu walked up from his desk and stood beside me, his face tranquil. The sun shone on his large brown eyes and made them transparent. Across the street a naked woman darted from a hut and quickly ducked into another.

"The rain must be a nuisance for these people," I said.

"It is good for the crops. It is a matter of Karma."

"And the wheel of Karma, just like the wheel of industrialization, never stops, Muthu?"

He nodded. "That is also Karma. Men think it is their duty to create industry. Some think it is their duty to make money. One must do one's duty."

It was simple. Like that. "And Ghosh?" I asked.

"Ghosh is also doing his duty. His illusion is no greater than Mr. Khemka's. They mistake the action of their senses for their own actions. It is all Maya."

"You talk like a mystic."

"No," Muthu said. "I am a very weak man." He looked away.

There was a sound of loud voices and Ghosh stormed out of Sheila's office.

"You will never get away with it!" He stormed across the room. I tried to intercept him but he walked past me, blind with rage. The next moment he was in the street and gone.

I laughed and turned towards Muthu, but the tranquillity of his face was broken with a streak of worry.

"I don't like this," he said. "It'll be advisable if you see Miss Khemka."

Sheila was still ruffled when I entered. "Who asked you to come in?" she scolded.

I said, "I'll go."

"No, don't leave yet. I have something to tell you. Sit down."

"This man Ghosh," she began, "you....this income tax thing." She stopped abruptly, undecided whether to continue. "Well, forget it," she said at last.

Muthu watched me closely as I came out. Poor man. I wished I had something to tell him. But I knew little more than he did. I could hear the rumblings of a distant storm but since there was very little I could do I saw no point in getting myself involved. But as later events proved, one does not choose one's involvement. The day came when I got involved anyway.

6

WITH THE coming of September the monsoon gave way to the sickly, sticky heat which precedes winter in north India. I had become quite accustomed to life in the office. You might even say I enjoyed it. I had finally been able to establish myself as an eccentric whose mediocrity assured suspicious fellow workers that no harm was intended. I did the work assigned to me and the volume increased gradually. There was enough to keep even the mediocre busy and Mr. Khemka believed in getting his money's worth.

When I was not at the office I loafed about the old city. A strange and half familiar exhilaration filled me as I walked through the tortuous streets jammed with shouting children. At least they were different from the crowd I worked with or met at Mr. Khemka's house.

Sometimes Mr. Khemka asked me about my social life. His interest in it puzzled me a bit in the beginning. I had no social life to speak of. I had only one life and it could be called by whatever name one wished. I told him as much, but my reply seemed to disappoint him. With measured paternalness he told me that to move up in India one needed good contacts and that such contacts could not be developed without a proper social life. I told him politely that I was not interested in moving up. A proper social life therefore was not quite necessary for me.

Mr Khemka and his daughter lived in a strange world through which I wandered occasionally like a sleepwalker without grasping what it was all about. The reason they attended so many gigantic parties and threw so many of their own, I first thought, was because they were occupied with making more money. Gradually, it dawned on me that they were also afraid of being alone. This was perhaps natural since they had always lived in a crowd and the women especially had little or nothing to do.

Sheila was an exception to this. She belonged to many worlds at the same time and I admired her for that. In all those months I would have liked to spend more time with her except that she invariably started talking about Babu and I didn't particularly enjoy that. I stuck

42

to vague generalities about Babu, giving her in driblets what she wanted in a torrent. But I knew that sooner or later it all would reach the same pool. And that was what happened one day in October when autumn was turning to winter and I was chafing to go for a walk in the gardens.

That was the day Professor White gave a talk. While I was wading through a pile of import licences the telephone rang. It was Arun. We had been together in Boston and he had kept in touch with me. He told me White was one of our old professors who used to look after foreign students. "Would I come?"

"I don't know. Are you going?"

"Yes. He was your professor, wasn't he? I think you ought to go." That is Arun: always respectful to the chiefs.

"I'll see," I said.

In the evening I went. I had nothing else to do. Somebody from the Ministry of Education introduced the professor. "We are fortunate," he said, "to have in our midst a representative of one of the finest universities in the world."

Neat little rows of moustached Indians listened to White's nonsense with pious attention. It was some kind of prattle about foreign student life in America. I was not listening, but here and there a phrase sent me racing back through the skeleton of dead years.

His very accent..... How often had I heard that accent in bars above the din of pinball machines. Only the bars were real and the men who lusted over the maids' breasts didn't pretend to be professors of economic history.

"Every foreign student is an ambassador of his country," the professor was saying. Arun winked across the aisle at me and I almost laughed; it was as if a mischievous statue had suddenly come to life. The thought that I had been an ambassador was perfectly hilarious. That was the usual dope they gave you. And what country had I represented? Kenya or England or India? The bartenders never considered me an ambassador. They knew I was another drinker, who deserved sympathy and that was all there was to know. They never asked me what I thought of the Five Year Plans or why I didn't hate Russia. They knew I was a nobody like them who only hated himself.

The question hour began. Somebody wanted to know the best university for econometrics in America. Somebody else asked about scholarships. It always came down to that. In India everything ended in seeking money.

"Is it true, Professor," said a woman somewhere behind me, "that many Indian students in America feel very lost?" She hesitated for a moment. "Some of them even commit suicide?"

I sat upright in my chair and whirled around. It was Sheila. She was huddled in a corner, blushing under the gaze of the audience.

I turned back to look at White. He was groping for words. Of course he could overcome the situation! Make any remark and have it believed.

"It is true," he finally began, "that sometimes the strain of adjustment on certain people proves unbearable. This even happens to the American student. But the foreign students offices in different universities make sure that strain is kept to a minimum...." He gave a detailed account of how social get-togethers were organised for the benefit of foreign students and how they were invited to American homes to spend holidays. But I wasn't listening.

The shock of Sheila's question had sent me careening on a totally different track. I was afraid, suddenly. Did she know? Could he have written just before he went for the drive? No, that wasn't possible. He had only a few minutes, according to June. He couldn't have written a letter in that time! He was in no fit condition to write, anyway. Had I given myself away? My mind raced back over the numerous conversations with Sheila. Had she just guessed by intuition? Fear does make people superstitious.

I tried to understand why I was afraid. It was nothing physical. They couldn't put me in prison. I feared something much worse—the abominable hands groping and probing into my own soul, ripping dry scars open and dipping into old wounds.

The dollar talk was followed by a dollar tea. I waited. I had to see Sheila. There was a big hand on my shoulder, twisting me around.

"Hi, Sindi,"

"Hullo Professor White."

"We miss you back at the office." He was the one who sent me the annual "thank-you-host" testimonial.

"How is Ruth?" Ruth was his secretary.

"Oh, fine, fine. Keen as ever. Got married last summer. Going to have a baby."

"Whose baby?" I asked. But White had a knack for not hearing what he didn't want to hear.

"You look tired," he said. It sounded phoney.

44

"We all have our private worries, Professor."

"Not falling in love, are you? I thought you were getting married. To what's-her-name ?"

"June," I said. "She left me."

"I'm sorry."

"It all evens out in the long run, Professor."

I was glad when somebody whisked him away. Sheila was just leaving the room. I hurriedly left. She waited on the pavement, watching for a taxi.

"Shall I call a cab for you ?" I asked, walking up to her.

She turned to face me but her eyes did not focus. She seemed preoccupied with other thoughts.

"Can we have a cup of tea somewhere before you go ?" I said.

"I don't mind." Her voice was faint and I had to strain to catch her answer.

We sat upstairs at Wengers where young executives have their business receptions. Except for two teenage girls, we were alone in the room. A crowd of workmen with tattered banners was gathered on the lawn across the road. They obviously were waiting for their leader. "All India Scavengers Union," the banners said.

"Why did you ask that question, Sheila?" I said when we had settled down to tea.

"Just out of curiosity. I had read it somewhere."

"It wasn't mere curiosity, Sheila. You know that as well as I do."

I waited, hoping she would say something. When she finally spoke it was not what I had expected.

"Did Babu say anything before he died?"

"No. He was quite dead when we found him."

"Was he smashed badly?"

I hesitated. I wondered if I could tell her what he looked like. The peeled face, the gaping hole where his eye had been.

"No." I lied. "He was all right. He just hit a rock and fell into a stream. We might have saved him if we had known where he had gone. But, Sheila," I said a little exasperated, "can't you forget about it? He might have died a worse death. And...." I had started to add that we all had to die one way or another. What does it matter if you are splattered on a rock or gasp away under a thrombosis? But it sounded hollow. I knew it was all right for me who had nothing to lose by

45

dying and whose death there was nobody to mourn. Sheila had loved Babu more than herself.

"Do you really believe I can forget it?"

"No." I said.

"Tell me why he died, Sindi! Please tell me why he died!" Her voice was almost drowned by a swell of cheers from the workers across the street, but I could not miss the painful plea. I noticed that the leader had arrived.

Tell her why he died? Why he died? I was afraid again. Did she suspect anything?

"What do you mean, Sheila? I've told you about the accident almost a dozen times. Surely, there is nothing very strange about a man dying in a car accident, is there?"

There was a long pause and then without lifting her eyes she said. "It wasn't an accident, Sindi." Her tone was very quiet and controlled.

So she knew? I could feel the sweat breaking in my armpits. Her face was a mask of sadness, without suspicion or reproach.

"Why do you say that, Sheila?" I asked as steadily as I could.

"His letters. There was a sudden change in the tone of his letters just before he died. They almost carried the message of his death. He seemed completely lost and alone. He never said it, but I know it had something to do with the girl."

A sob choked off her speech. She was trying hard to restrain herself. I reached out and tried to take her hand, but she moved it away. She didn't want sympathy. After a while she continued.

"Oh, God! I wish I had died in his place. Nobody would miss me. But Babu! He was always so alive! I will never think of him as dead. If only he could be brought back of life, he would be so happy, happy and gay as he always was!"

She cried freely now. Tears rolled down her cheeks and she wiped at them with her trembling hands. I might have been cynical, but I could recognize pain when it was thrust in my face.

"I'm sorry, Sheila. I am really sorry."

The crowd across the street was quiet. They were listening to the gesticulating leaders planted on the shabby platform. I wondered how many of them had jobs. But they seemed happy, all the same. It was "fun" listening to the leader. They could talk about it later. They

46

looked on impassively as his hands went up in a gesture of frustration, seeking once and for all to dismember his personal sorrows, searching endlessly for the road to Parliament and then to the Cabinet. He believed, just as Sheila believed, that he could be happy if things were different. I continued the futile attempt to reassure her.

"You have your work, your father to take care of, your new factories to worry about, your money to invest."

"What is all this money for? I don't need it."

"But your father does."

"Yes, but he is selfish."

"We are all selfish, Sheila. Babu was selfish, too. Only he was innocent enough to let his selfishness destroy him. Your father is clever."

"Father even refused to read Babu's letters. How could anyone be so brutal?"

"You kept all his letters?"

"I have some right here." She opened her bag and took out a frayed envelope and handed it to me. George Washington's stern countenance presided over Babu's boyish hand. Babu's ghost had caught up with me again. This time with an old envelope full of letters. I took out the one on top. It had been written six months before his death. He had not yet snatched June away from me.

"Dear Didi," it began.

"You haven't written to me for so long that I almost feel angry. I have half a mind not to write to you until I hear from you.

"I am sad today, Didi. We had an exam this morning and I didn't do well. I never seem to do well in these exams. They are very strict here. If I don't do well this year they might ask me to leave. How could I show my face to anyone if that happens? The humiliation would be unbearable."

I wished they had asked him to leave, that I hadn't interfered. He might still be living.

"In India when I messed up an exam, I always talked it over with you and forgot about it. But here I have no one, no one at all. Of course, Sindi is always willing to listen to me. But he is so terribly cynical I am afraid he will make fun of me if I took my small problems to him."

47

He splashed acid into the right wound. I could see his sad slouching figure against the snow-swept windows while I drank whisky and soda. I, who had prided myself on detachment and courage, hadn't seen his grief when it writhed two feet from me. God, how vain I had been!

"Besides the exam there are many other things. I can't even talk to you about them. Everywhere I turn I am faced with my deficiencies. When I consider how much you all expect of me, my heart sinks. Father writes to me every week. He expects so much of me. Oh, Didi, I don't think I can ever fulfil his expectations. I don't know what to do. Don't show this letter to Father. He would get angry, I'm afraid. Write to me often, please. You are all that I have left."

Later he thought June was all that he had left. It was this selfpity that had killed him, but I couldn't explain that to Sheila. She thought Babu had been the victim. He was, but she accused the wrong assailant.

The next letter was written three months later.

"I have bad news for you, Didi. For weeks now I have been wondering how to break it to you. I am getting married. I have gone through weeks of turmoil before reaching this decision. At last I have found enough courage to marry the girl I love. And yet sometimes at night I wake up with Father's raving image before me and all my strength drains out of me.

"Don't imagine that June is the ordinary sort of American girl that other Indians marry. She has got intellect and beauty that I can't hope to find elsewhere. And above all she loves me. She loves me more than anybody she has ever known. Sindi has also known her and thinks highly of her.

"The school has closed for the summer and Sindi has gone away I don't know where. A shadow has come between us. I am afraid he is angry with me. I don't know why."

Angry indeed. He ought to have known better than that. A man sentenced to death doesn't feel angry; he only wishes for a quick release. It had not been anger that had raged within me as I sweated in impersonal laboratories that lonely summer. It wasn't anger that I

48

had sought to assuage but a release from suffering and the desire that caused it.

"Please break this news gently to Father. I don't have the courage to write to him myself. Tell him I beg his forgiveness on bended knees. Tell him I'll do all he wishes but please don't make me leave June. I can't live without her. Sindi laughed at me when I said this to him but I know that if I lose her I shall certainly die."

He had found another wound. Yes, I hadn't quite believed him. I couldn't believe it was all that serious. Engrossed as I was in my own suffering, I hadn't quite believed the stakes that Babu was playing for.

"Did you tell your father ?" I asked.

"Yes, I had to." Sheila said. "He was furious. For two days he neither slept nor ate. Then he sent off a cable threatening to cut Babu off from his property if he married June."

"And Babu replied that he would choose June if it came to a choice."

"How did you know?"

"He told me."

"Did he also tell you that June gave him more love in two months than his father had in twenty years?"

"No," I said. "But I knew that. June knew how to give, if only because she was afraid of being selfish."

"Did you know her well?"

"Yes."

"What was she like?"

"Tall and slim, with blonde hair and large blue eyes." I described her like an automobile: light grey with a radio and heater, or red over black with white sidewalls.

"I meant inside," Sheila said, pointing to her breast where the soul is supposed to reside.

"Beautiful."

"I don't believe it. Read the third letter yourself and you will know." Sheila sounded almost vicious.

"Dear Didi," it began.

"I fear I am going mad. June is driving me mad and she doesn't even know it. Her behaviour has suddenly changed. Outwardly it is still the same and yet I know that something has snapped between us.

"At times I hate her. Only I love her more passionately later on. I don't know what has come over her just two weeks before the marriage. We used to meet each other every day and we still do but there is a shadow in her face which tells me she doesn't love me anymore. When I ask her, she just laughs and tells me I am having hallucinations. At times the horrible suspicion that she might be carrying on with another man almost drives me to the point of madness. If I could only be sure, Sheila, if I could only be *sure*. Perhaps I am wrong and this is all a big mistake. I pray to God I am mistaken. This is the first time I have turned to God in many months.

"I wish Sindi were here. I wish I could tell him about my problems. I can still perhaps get his address and write to him. I'm sure he will help me. He probably knows June much better than I do. If only he would, for once, not laugh at me and give some advice.

"I'll close now, Didi. I could go on indefinitely, but I don't want to tax your patience. Perhaps you don't want to see my face either. Please forgive me."

For a minute everything appeared misty and blurred. I folded the letter and put it back in the envelope with the others. "At times the horrible suspicion that she might be carrying on with another man almost drives me to the point of madness." If only I had known what he was going through. I should have guessed, but I had been blinded by my own detachment.

"What do you think of her now ?" Sheila asked.

"She was beautiful and humane," I said.

"I suppose you were also infatuated with her."

"I suppose I was," I said, "but one is always infatuated with only what is humane and beautiful."

"How can there be anything beautiful about a woman who goes about laying snares for young boys?"

"You are not fair to what she was, Sheila. I am sure you would have liked her. And then don't forget that codes of morality differ from country to country. Girls do certain things in America that women would never do here. That doesn't mean they are wicked."

"She was a harlot and a witch," Sheila said venomously, "and she killed my brother."

I gave up. There was no point in going into all that. Sheila was going to believe what she wanted to believe, anyway. I was tired and depressed. The mild, mellow beauty of the twilights outside saddened me more. I wished I belonged to the Scavengers Union and had never set my eyes on Sheila or Mr Khemka or their silly, ice-cream gobbling crowd.

I tried once more.

"It was his innocence that killed him, Sheila. Innocence concocted by you and your father. He lived in a world of dreams, in a world with sculpture in drawing rooms. In the end, the hard facts of life proved stronger than his flimsy world of dreams. His death could have been heroic. But the pity of it was that the dreams were not even his own— they were products of the turbid flotsam of a rotting social class he was supposed to perpetuate."

"It was for his own good !" Sheila said and her eyes blazed.

"Your father probably said the same thing. And, of course, your father wouldn't admit that he sent Babu to America so he would come back and add that much more weight to your family's social status. He could talk to friends at the club about his foreign-returned son."

"Father wanted him to be respectable," Sheila said. "Where is the harm in that? Babu was his son. He loved him!"

"Yes, he did. But not as a son. Your father loved him like a factory. Babu was a pawn in your father's hands with no will or life of his own. That's why he couldn't bear the thought of Babu marrying June. It didn't fit in his plans. He wanted to marry Babu to a fat Marwari girl whose dowry might bring him half a dozen new factories."

"You don't understand," Sheila said. "You don't understand India and you don't understand Indian traditions."

"I talk with a different accent and you think I don't know India. But answer this. Why did your father object to Babu's marriage?"

"It is just not done. You...you marry in your own caste. A foreigner just doesn't fit in our homes."

51

"Why? Why not?"

"They don't know the language, the customs. Their religion is different."

"We all know English, don't we?" I asked. "Even now we are speaking English, aren't we? As for religion, I thought Hindus prided themselves on their tolerance."

"They do."

"But it doesn't work out in practice, is that it?"

"Yes! Yes! Yes! That's it! Why ask me if you know everything?"

"Don't get angry, Sheila. I really want to know. Foreigners don't fit in our homes because we don't want them to fit in, isn't that the reason?"

"June wouldn't have been acceptable to us, that is all I know," Sheila said. And then she added with an air of stubborn finality that left little to be said: "She wasn't virtuous."

"How do you know she was not virtuous?"

"All I know is that she was not a virgin. Babu told me himself."

Her use of word "virgin" surprised me and again I found myself wondering how much she knew. "Is that all?" I asked, and when she nodded I laughed.

"So you think one of these Marwari girls is really superior merely because of a silly membrane between her legs?"

Sheila blushed. She tried to hide her embarrassment by pretending to blow her nose.

"I am sorry, Sheila. I forgot I was talking with you."

I was embarrassed at her discomfiture. One just didn't talk like that to a girl like Sheila.

"I think I should be going home," she said.

I paid the bill. While we were leaving the tea house she stumbled on the stairs. Instinctively I caught her around the waist. For an instant she stood pressed against me. I felt her warm breath on my neck. My hand was firmly clasped on her bare waist just above her sari. Then she turned and moved down the staircase gracefully.

In the taxi she turned and said, "You have not answered my question. Why did Babu die?'

"It was an accident Sheila." I repeated.

"Honestly." It was a statement and a question at the same time.

"Yes, honestly." After all I could not honestly say that it was not an accident.

52

"It had nothing to do with June?"

I hesitated for a moment. Then I lied.

"No."

I watched her go into the house. Her step had the unusual grace that only Indian girls have. For a moment I wanted to call her back. Then I changed my mind.

7

LIKE A schoolboy I counted the house numbers as I went down the street.

Sixty-eight, sixty-six, sixty-four....It was almost a countdown of my courage. After three days of illness I was once again on my feet. The illness had left me pale and exhausted, but I was glad to get out of my room.

Three days of life had passed, leaving a taste of death in my mouth. I could almost feel my chin sagging and my heart coming to a standstill. But now, as I walked towards June's house, another feeling possessed me. I was afraid: I was afraid of getting involved with June.

The morning after the night in the country June had come to see me on her way to work. Both Karl and I were surprised at her entrance. Karl wore nothing except a pair of drawers. I was still in bed. She walked straight into my bedroom and giggled when she saw me tucked up in bed. I smelled of sweat and medicines and I felt awkward when she put her hand on my forehead and sat down on the bed. She tweaked my nose and said, "How is the little brown Indian today?"

I said I was all right. I was feeling miserable but what was the point in telling her that? She brushed my hair back from my forehead and told me I would soon be well. She didn't know what she was talking about but it was nice of her to say so. She had brought some flowers for me which she wanted to put near the bed. We didn't have a vase in the house but Karl managed to produce an old bottle of Vat 69 from somewhere which served admirably as a flower vase. Against the blue patch of sky carved out by the window the tulips

53

seemed more alive than I was. A Salvation Army band would have convinced me that I was dying.

June left as suddenly as she had come, but she promised to return in the evening. After she was gone Karl removed his trousers once again and sat down near me. For some reason he never wore trousers in the house.

"I never knew you had a girl, you old rogue," he said grinning. "How long have you known her?"

I looked at my watch and calculated.

"Twelve hours and forty minutes," I said.

"You seem to have worked your charm very well in the short time."

I think that was the moment when I first grew afraid of getting involved. So long as they ignored me, things were all right. It was only when they thought me charming that the whole trouble started. "I don't think it is a matter of charm, Karl. June takes pity on all sick people."

"There is very little difference between love and pity. One is only marginally less repulsive than the other. They both lead to sex."

I said I could see his point but I didn't quite agree with him. Personally, I didn't find them so much repulsive as *overpowering*.

He asked me what I meant. I said I didn't know exactly but I had always felt it. Love was like a debt that you had to return sooner or later. And if you didn't you felt very uncomfortable.

Karl laughed and slapped me on the leg. "You Indians have got strange theories. One of these days you will all go nuts, I can assure you."

He got up and went into the bathroom. I heard him whistling a popular tune and then he came back all lathered up, his broken mirror in one hand and razor in the other. Good old Karl. He thought I needed company.

Karl finished shaving. Blood oozed slowly out of numerous cuts and he dabbed at his face with a towel.

"The trouble with me is I am too good looking for the world of those crazy women," he said. "They run you down and there is nothing left for you to do except let yourself be loved. It takes the entire fun out of the game. I want to hunt down my own women." Karl sounded rather flippant, so I said, "You still have other men's wives to hunt down. And what about the movie stars—Marilyn Monroe, for example?"

"They disgust me."

"That is all the more reason for you to hunt them down."

"You know, I really have no guts. Every time I have an affair, I promise myself it will be the last one. But the same thing happens over and over again. Some lonely wretch takes me home and pulls me on top of her. I feel her lusty naked body and in a moment all my vows are forgotten. I go through the motions and I hear her moan with pleasure under me. And I know it is I, Karl, who is giving her this pleasure. She wants me. That is when the knot is tied, another affair begins. I can't even untie that knot myself. I just don't have the guts."

"You have a kind heart, Karl. You pity your women. You suffer in their place. You are almost a martyr."

"Yeah?" Karl said laughing. "I think I'll buy myself a huge cross and drag it around the streets when I go out."

"They'll stone you, I'm afraid."

Karl got up. "Time for me to run along to the labs," he said. "Give your friend my regards when you see her. Tell her I like her hair."

"You might tell her yourself, she'll be here this evening."

" I won't be in this evening. As a matter of fact, I'm sleeping at a friend's house."

"Another affair, eh!"

Karl sighed and went out.

When he was gone I found myself thinking of June. I wondered if she had been charmed by me as Karl had said. It didn't quite seem possible, although it was strange the way she showed up again so soon. I felt depressed, what with the illness and so many drugs. Lying there in the bed I wondered in what way, if any, did I belong to the world that roared beneath my apartment window. Somebody had begotten me without a purpose and so far I had lived without a purpose, unless you could call the search for peace a purpose. Perhaps I felt like that because I was a foreigner in America. But then, what difference would it have made if I had lived in Kenya or India or any other place for that matter! It seemed to me that I would still be a foreigner. My foreignness lay within me and I couldn't leave myself behind wherever I went. I hadn't felt like that when my uncle was living. It wasn't that I loved him very much or anything—as a matter of fact we rarely exchanged letters—but the thought that he moved about in that small house on the outskirts of Nairobi gave me a feeling of having an anchor. After his death the security was destroyed. Now I suppose I existed only for dying; so far as far I knew everybody else did the same thing. It was sad, nonetheless.

June came that evening as she had promised She was in high spirits and her smooth cheeks were flushed with excitement. She sat down beside me on the bed and put her hand in mine.

"Are you feeling better?"

I nodded

"You don't talk much, do you?"

I said I had nothing to talk about.

"Tell me all you did today."

"Karl and I had a long discussion on love."

"And what did you decide?"

"Nothing much," I said. In these things one didn't decide anything as one hardly knew the facts.

June got up and switched on the radio. Jazz filled the darkening room. Suddenly she stretched out her arms and burst into a dance. Her dance didn't have any steps, rules or conventions so far as I could make out. It was rhythm twirled on a potter's block. I could see the muscles of her thigh flex through the tight skirt and yet the impression she gave was not of vulgarity but that of youth. Like a bow she bent forward, her hair falling over her face revealing the pink, long neck with just a few curls covering the tender skin. Then the arrow was released and the bow relaxed. The hair fell back revealing a flushed smiling face. As she twirled around, her small breasts were silhouetted against the window. It all filled me with a sudden desire to hold her, to pass my arm around that narrow waist and tell her that I wanted to live. I wanted to pull her down beside me and physically possess her, irrespective of what the consequences might be. I don't know how long her dance lasted. Five minutes or ten minutes or half an hour. In those brief minutes she revealed to me all that I was not and couldn't hope to be. Maybe that is why I later fell in love with her even as I struggled to remain uninvolved.

The radio man switched to the hourly news bulletin; the way he began one almost expected him to announce that the world had suddenly stopped during the last hour. June slipped beside me on the bed, and leaning over me she kissed me as she might have kissed a sick child. I could feel her warm breath on my cheek and her hair fell into my eyes.

I could hear her breathing next to me while I lay awkwardly like a log, feeling embarrassed because I smelt so awfully of drugs and sweat. All of a sudden she straightened and took my hand.

"Can you get up?" she asked excitedly. "I want you to come and watch the sunset."

I gathered my strength and got out of bed. I lived in the poorer part of Boston. Westward from my window there was a vast plateau of ramshackle apartment houses beyond which the river meandered noiselessly to the sea. But far beyond all this, far beyond the reach of man's greed, the autumn sun went down in majestic splendour. A gigantic golden fleece stretched across the horizon from one end to the other. Mauve tufts of cloud crowded along its middle, and beneath it the sky was green. For a long while we stood there watching the blazing ball and its surrounding brightness fall from the air. When it was dark June said, "I must go now. Mother will be getting worried. You must come and see us when you are well."

And now I was well, counting the house numbers with fear in my heart. Twenty-two...twenty...no...eighteen. They were demolishing No. 20.

Number ten was a small house resplendent with fresh paint. Little heaps of grass lay at random like a throw of dice; somebody had been mowing the lawn. The smell of drying grass hit my lungs and instinctively I shrank before it; I had been told I was allergic to hay. A spaniel sat disconsolately before the shining door. I had to step over him to ring the knocker. Mrs. Blyth opened the door.

"Ah, you must be Sindi," she shrieked ecstatically. "Come in, come on in."

Before I could move, the dog rushed between my legs and climbed all over the old lady.

"Oh, get off, you silly beast! I say off with you! Monsieur Pilot!" Mrs. Blyth scolded. But Monsieur Pilot's affection knew no bounds. He would have gone on muzzling the old lady had not June arrived and given him a resounding slap on the ear.

In her yellow cotton dress June looked girlish and beautiful. Her mouth seemed fuller than before and the large eyes were like a lake after rain.

The small living room was warm and comfortable. June introduced me to her mother.

"I know. I know," chirped the old lady. "I had one look at his big brown eyes and I knew it was him." A moment of embarrassed silence followed while I stared at my nails, but the old lady was talkative.

"What part of India are you from, Sindi? You don't mind my calling you Sindi, do you? If you do, you just have to let me know."

"I'm from Kenya, Mrs. Blyth," I said.

"Can what?"

"Kenya. It is in Africa."

"You are not from Africa, are you? But you don't look like a nigger." The old lady looked puzzled and alarmed at the same time.

"He's not a Negro, mother." June said with a touch of irritation. "A lot of Indians have settled in Kenya for business reasons."

"Are you in business, Sindi?" The old lady continued. She apparently wasn't satisfied with my credentials.

"No. My father was."

"What does he do now?"

"He's dead."

"Oh, I'm sorry," said Mrs. Blyth. I had a feeling she was genuinely sorry. "I bet your mother misses you very much."

"No, she doesn't, she is dead, too."

This really hit the cockles of Mrs. Blyth's kind heart. I almost expected her to fly at me and weep on my shoulder. Even June appeared visibly moved but she said nothing. I hadn't told her anything about myself.

"Mama went to India last year," June said trying to retrieve the conversation.

"Oh," I said, "where all did you go?"

An opportunity to talk about her visit seemed to revive Mrs. Blyth.

"We started at Calcutta. You see, we were coming from Bangkok. Then we went to Benaras. I saw a Raja's wedding there... ".

Mrs Blyth rattled along. I looked around the room. A huge photograph of a bearded man stood over the fireplace. He probably was June's father. June sat in the corner, her hands folded in her lap waiting for her mother to stop. Monsieur Pilot suddenly woke up, gave everybody a perfunctory glance, and went back to sleep. Mrs Blyth had reached Agra. The Taj, she said, was wonderful in the moonlight.

Once we had settled down in the comfortable high-backed chairs my fear returned. Was I getting involved? Could this be the beginning of uncontrollable events? Perhaps not. I had sat in many living rooms before. But this time there was a difference. June was different. Something stirred inside me when I looked at her. Perhaps I was getting old. I would be twenty-five next month. Was involvement inevitable with age?

After Mrs. Blyth was finished I asked her how she had liked her trip to India.

"It was wonderful. I want to show you my slides after dinner. I must go now and have a look at my roast."

After she was gone I pointed to the photograph and asked, "Is that your father?"

"Yes, in a way. Daddy and Mama separated long ago."

"Where is he now?"

"Last we heard from him, he was in Mexico. He paints."

I asked her if she missed him. "Yes," she said. "I would have liked to have had a father; but it doesn't matter much now. You get used to things."

She apparently didn't want to talk about her father. Silence hit the room once more. I felt weak and at peace with myself. Just sitting there and watching the hands of the clock filled me with peace. There was nothing I wanted to talk about, nothing I wanted to hear. Amidst the clink of pots and pans, Mrs. Blyth kept up her pleasant chatter from the kitchen, but neither of us answered; she didn't expect any answer. The smell of roast turkey crept into the room like an uninvited child whenever she opened the oven. This was what she had probably enjoyed most in her life—opening and shutting ovens, feeding other people until they were fit to burst. For a month after her husband left her did she cry while she cooked for her little daughter. Or may be it was a year, may be even now she sometimes cried. How long does it take to mend a broken heart? I didn't know it then.

Suddenly I became conscious of June's gaze. When I looked at her she smiled.

"What are you always thinking?" she said.

"Nothing. I only appear to be thinking."

"I hope you are not bored."

"Not at all. As a matter of fact I am enjoying myself. I like this house, it is different from mine."

"In what way?"

"My flat has no personality. There are no sounds, no smells; it is like an inn, you walk in and you walk out, just as if you were in an unfamiliar town."

"Why don't you move in with a family?"

"I didn't say I preferred a house with a personality. I am happy as I am. Some people must live in an inn, you know."

"Isn't that rather selfish?"

Her remark made me a little uncomfortable. She continued, "I'm afraid I don't quite understand you. What will you do if you get married?"

I said I didn't know what I would do but at the moment the question didn't arise as I didn't believe in marriage.

"You don't believe in marriage?" she said slowly.

"I thought you got married or you didn't marry, it never struck me there were beliefs involved."

I said there was always a belief involved if you dug deep enough. I didn't want to talk about all this but now I was in the thick of it and had to talk about something. After a while she said.

"But why don't you believe in marriage?"

I said I didn't quite know except that whatever I had seen so far in life seemed to indicate that marriage was more often a lust for possession than anything else. People got married just as they bought new cars. And then they gobbled each other up.

"But marriage is also love, isn't it!" June said.

I said I imagined it was since everybody said so, but as far as I was concerned, love that wanted to possess was more painful than no love at all.

"One should be able to love without wanting to possess," I said. "Otherwise you end up by doing a lot more harm than good. One should be able to detach oneself from the object of one's love."

June said, "I can't. I don't think anyone can unless he is a saint."

I kept quiet. I supposed she was right. After a pause she spoke again.

"Have you always been that way? I mean, have you always had the same view of life?"

"No. Somebody taught it to me."

I still remembered Kathy's little figure waving to me from the carriage door as her train finally steamed out of Paddington station.

"Did, one of your Sadhus teach it to you ?"

"No," I laughed. "It was a girl in London."

"Did you love her?"

"No. I had only wanted to possess her."

"And you suffered because of it?"

"Yes If I had loved her I wouldn't have hurt myself."

"Did she leave you?"

"She had to leave me; she was married."

Even after several years, somewhere in the labyrinth of my consciousness the wound still bled. I felt sad and perhaps showed it.

"I'm sorry," June said kindly. "I shouldn't have made you talk about it."

"It's nothing. One can't always forget one's past."

Monsieur Pilot got up and crept up to us, yawning and slobbering. He had no past.

Suddenly Mrs. Blyth called from the kitchen. "The dinner is ready, let's eat."

We ate and ate and ate until there was nothing left to do but drop to the floor and go to sleep.

But Mrs. Blyth had other plans for us.

"Now," she chirped, "we'll go to the living room and watch my show." The show, as it turned out, consisted of about a million slides of her package trip around the world.

June and I sat side by side in the darkened room. Mrs. Blyth sat a little apart. Between us the automatic slide projector hummed like a mischievous insect. Mrs. Blyth rattled off her cut-and-dried commentary, perhaps for the hundredth time.

"San Francisco Airport. That's our group." I looked at a crowd of grey, bedraggled, lonely people who had suddenly realised that life had left them by the wayside.

"Honolulu," shouted Mrs. Blyth, like a train attendant in a children's park. Everybody had a garland; everybody smiled; only the eyes betrayed the emptiness.

The scene shifted to Japan. Glittering shops on the Ginza... a parody of Mrs. Blyth in a Kimono...Pagodas in Bangkok had been put in the projector upside down... a sea of sampans.

"I liked that shot of sampans, Mrs. Blyth," I said. But she wasn't listening. She fumbled with the slides and talked to herself like a child. Suddenly she cried, "And now to India!"

"Do you recognise them?"

Two naked children stood in the middle of a filthy street. I winced involuntarily.

"Yes," I said.

"Have you been to India?" June asked.

"No."

"How come? Don't you want to?"

"I do. I have never had the money."

A magnificent shot of the Hooghly at sunset followed. Then the slums near Sealdah. I wondered why tourists were so fond of photographing other people's misery. As I watched the putrid humanity crowding over each other I was conscious of being hurt. A mixture of sadness and rage grew within me. There was something obviously unjust in all this even though one couldn't lay one's finger on it. Mrs Blyth rattled off a string of platitudes about India's poverty and what American missionaries had done to improve conditions. She had probably read that stuff in one of those guide books which sold for $ 1.95 in the corner drug-store.

Even in the dark I was conscious of June's gaze. Her hand crept out of her lap and gently caressed my arm. Then she slipped her little soft hand into mine and gently squeezed it. From the corner of my eye I could see her bending towards me.

"I'm sorry," she whispered. "All this must be horrid for you. Don't be angry with Mama. She doesn't mean anything."

Her hair brushed against my cheek. It smelt of shampoo and I was sorry when she moved away. It struck me that it had been ages since I had smelt a woman's head. For three long years I had not felt the need but now, suddenly, I wanted to take that head in my hands and cover it with kisses. I felt uncomfortable. I told myself that I didn't want to get involved.

A crowd of gesticulating Bengalis jostled in front of a hideous statue of Kali.

"One thing I don't like at all about Hinduism is their nonsense about idols. It just isn't human," said Mrs. Blyth.

I looked at her with amusement this time. June's fingers were laced with mine. All my rage had drained out. Only sadness remained. But even a sad man could laugh.

Mrs. Blyth moved on to Benaras. Photographs of the Raja's wedding seemed endless. "I don't want to get involved." I repeated to myself. Everywhere I turned I saw involvement. How long could I stay free! The pain of earlier years had taught me wisdom but I didn't know if I could depend upon it. The commitment had already been made the moment I had seen June at the dance. Now it was only a matter of time. Our hands would soon give place to our bodies and then the worst will come; our souls will get involved. It was only a matter of time.

It had been different when I didn't know the outcome. Now I knew it only too well. I could already see the death struggle of our souls as each of us tried to claim his own destiny. I could taste the tears of bitterness and failure. I could see the lengthening shadows in unlighted rooms while outside the evening turned to twilight and twilight into darkness. I could smell the decay of love, the sudden realisation that the end had begun. And worse, the fear that there might never be another beginning. The hand that so lovingly held mine would perhaps some day ache to hit me. I wasn't afraid of getting hurt, but to hurt June would have been unbearable. I could avoid the tears and the lengthening shadows if I only had the strength to act on what I knew was right. I might also have saved Babu had I possessed the courage to drop that lovely hand and walk out into the night.

But I didn't have the courage.

I didn't have the courage to say no when June said we should go to Cape Cod to spend my birthday.

Under the midday sun the beach was almost white. On the farthest tip of the beach two dots moved almost imperceptibly. Karl had joined us at the last minute. He said he was sick of the city; it reminded him too much of his last affair. The other dot was Arun. He had not joined us at all. We had run into him outside the supermarket and he had asked us for a short lift to the Boston Common. When we found he was merely going to sit there for the rest of the day, we dragged him along. He didn't have to think.

When the day warmed up June asked me to come and swim with her. I didn't particularly want to, but when she said she had been aching to swim with me all morning, I had no choice but to go along with her. We swam far out into the sea until I could hardly see the beach. I felt like a big fish. In spite of the warm sun the water was cold and I shivered everytime I stopped splashing. We didn't talk while we swam but I imagine June just liked the feeling of being two.

63

After a while I turned back and June followed me. When I came out of the water my teeth were chattering. Laughing, June threw a towel around my shoulders and dried me hurriedly. Then we lay down on the beach and for a while I slept.

When I woke up it was all very quiet. Arun and Karl had not yet returned.

June was so still beside me that she might have been asleep. In her bikini she seemed to have walked right out of the pages of a woman's magazine. She was pretty and graceful like a cat. I looked at her small round breasts and the gentle slope of her belly. She didn't arouse me sexually. Yet I wanted to possess her as I had never wanted to possess anyone before. The thought of possessing her had haunted me ever since that night in the woods. In the warm sunshine my tenderness—all the love that I had received in my life—reached out and enveloped her. I wanted to take her in my arms and tell her I wanted her. But that would have been fatal. As long as we didn't openly express our feelings there was still hope. I might get that new project in California; after all, it was not such a remote possibility. Chance might intervene at the last moment and provide us a pretext to break up what we were about to start: in the last resort one had to depend upon chance.

Suddenly June sat up and took off her dark glasses.

"I thought you were sleeping," I said.

"I wasn't, I was thinking about you."

I kept quiet. Then she said, "What did you do on your last birthday?"

I tried to recollect. What had I done? While I tried to remember, it struck me that men who led such ordinary lives as I must have difficulty in recalling the details of any one particular day. Then I remembered. Come to think of it, I had done nothing in particular. Karl and I had sat in the apartment drinking martinis. He had failed an exam that morning and for some reason I was feeling depressed myself. Birthdays always depress me; I don't know why. Towards evening we ran out on gin and ended up in one of those beatnik joints in Brighton. We had stayed there almost until midnight, buying each other drinks until everybody was staring at us. Finally, to top it off, Karl had stood up on the chair and made some silly speech about how it was his friend's birthday and could somebody give him a present. They had all laughed, not because Karl said anything funny but because they wanted to feel they were having a gay time.

"And then, coming home, Karl got sick in the subway. I didn't know whether to laugh or help him. I laughed, I guess."

"I didn't know you could laugh, too."

"I can if I'm drunk enough."

The dots appeared again on the horizon. On the vast beach they looked like a couple of lost adventurers in a movie.

"There they are," I said to June. Shading her eyes with her hand she gazed at them for a long while.

"Arun is a strange sort of man, isn't he?" June asked.

"I don't know what you mean by strange. To me he seems perfectly normal."

"I mean he never talks. And he gives you the feeling he knows everything. I don't like such men.

I said, "Why do you end up by liking or disliking people? Can't you just be neutral and take a man for what he is?"

"How can that be? We all have our likes and dislikes. Everybody has them. Don't you have any?"

I thought it over, then I said, "As far as I know I don't."

June pouted her mouth and said she was a woman and she had to have her likes and dislikes. Then she went on to say something about her intuition.

She said, "Take your case for example. I know nothing about you, yet I intuitively feel that you are a noble person and one could perhaps love you. I know nearly as much about Arun but I don't feel the same way about him."

All this embarrassed me. I always feel very awkward if somebody hints at love. To divert her conversation I said that Arun was quite likable in fact. He never said wonderful things about people, but then he never told a lie either. Then, looking at the approaching couple, she said.

"And what do you think of Karl?"

"Karl is different. You know he is lying and you don't seem to notice. Anyway, he only lies to himself. You know he will never keep those austerity measures he keeps on promising himself, but in his case it really does not matter."

"I thought you were a great one for keeping fast on resolutions."

It was funny the way she said it and I laughed. I said I didn't know whether I was a great one for keeping resolutions or not but, if I stuck to my resolutions, it was only because the pain of breaking them was too unbearable. Then I added.

"But in the case of Karl it is never a resolve in the first place. His resolutions are only directed at an emotional release for the moment. What for others can be a matter of life and death is just an expression of a vague sort of disgust for Karl. Today he is without a girl. In a month he will be sleeping with somebody. And yet the Karl you see now will be essentially the same as the Karl you will find then. Events hit him and they are bounced back. They never seem to get lodged in him."

Neither of us spoke for a while. Then she said, "With you it is different, isn't it?"

"What is different?"

"The making of resolutions. For you it is a matter of life and death?"

I said I didn't know since I wasn't conscious of having made any resolutions. I had wanted detachment but I didn't quite know what kind of resolutions were necessary to achieve it. At this point she started giggling. Then she leaned over and kissed me saying that I was a funny brown Indian. All this surprised me as I had assumed that we were having a serious conversation. But in a way I was glad to stop talking about myself.

Karl and Arun were very near now. "Look at Arun," I cried. The sight he presented was indeed miserable. Apparently he had gone for a swim with all his clothes on. He looked like a rat who had barely been saved from drowning. June had one look at him and she burst into laughter. In that brief moment perhaps she liked him.

"I'm hungry," Karl bellowed sullenly when he saw the lunch basket.

Many times, even now, in spring or autumn, when the weather is neither cold nor hot, the quiet peaceful beauty of that New England beach comes back to me, resting against a rock with ankles crossed, eating chicken salad sandwiches while the sea breathed quietly like a sleeping god. A little to our right a group of children in colourful trousers had appeared with a baseball bat. Each of us sat there munching sandwiches, lost in his own thoughts. And nobody was entirely separate from the group. There was a temporary bond of love between us. We knew it wouldn't last long, but the short while I was on that beach I forgot my strangeness, my loneliness, even my search for detachment. The sea struck me with humility. A bomber formation flew into the empty spaces of the sky pointing towards the eternal. The papers said there was trouble brewing in Berlin. One couldn't remain proud for long in those surroundings.

Arun took off his shirt and his vest. I noticed how thin he was and yet his body was beautifully made. Karl's sullenness had gradually ebbed away giving place to a wild sort of hilarity.

Another bomber formation went past, leaving a streak of sound in the blue sky.

"There is trouble in Berlin." Karl said noncommittally.

"Are you worried?" June said.

"No. Why should I be worried? I have abandoned Europe."

"It just seems unfair that people should have no say at all in a decision that might soon bring them death."

"Well, man never decides his own death, does he?" Arun said.

Karl almost shouted: "You Indians and your mealy mouthed philosophies! The trouble with you is you have never known war. If you were bombed every night for a year, why, even a month, I would like to see how many of you would still go around preaching the Bhagwad Gita."

"Not many preach the Gita even as it is," I said.

June laughed and lay down again. Her belly tightened and then relaxed. She was like a cat.

Karl frowned at the baseball players. He was itching to insult somebody. The bombers had probably hurt his European vanity. He turned to Arun once again.

"You Indians would bow down to the first man who comes along anyway. I don't know who put that non-violence, non-cooperation, non-nothing stuff in your heads."

"Nobody did. It only stands to reason. Nobody can rule you if you don't accept him as a ruler, if you don't cooperate."

"But what do you gain by non-cooperating except a couple of tears from some sentimental fools. You lose your freedom all the same, don't you? You can't go home again, your son can't study what he wants, your kids are snatched away and sent to kindergarten communes. Whether you cooperate or not you lose your freedom, can't you see that?"

Arun was silent for a long time. Then he quietly said, as if he were talking to himself. "But you are never free, Karl. How can anybody take away your freedom when you never had it in the first place? All freedom is illusion. You had no choice in your birth nor do you even choose your death. And in between is a vast expanse of lawless sands that pile up where the wind blows."

June had been listening quietly so far. Suddenly she sat up and said, "But you can always choose your death. You can always kill yourself."

"That is not freedom, it only shows the lack of it. Suicide is the end of a battered old road, not the beginning of a new one."

"If everything is beyond control then how do you suppose we live from day to day?"

Arun said dreamily. "Random events happen around you forcing you to make decisions propelling you on through life. It is only our vanity that makes us imagine that we are leading our own destiny." Then looking at June he said. "Have we come to this beach by choice? Aren't you here because you like Sindi and not because you made a choice?"

"Yes, but I have chosen to like Sindi. You have chosen to come with us rather than go to the Common."

"That is where your illusion comes in," Arun smiled. He had a beautiful smile.

"That is where your illusion comes in," he repeated. "I haven't chosen to come here any more than you. My loneliness is merely the obverse of your love. In reality neither loneliness nor love exists. Your past has driven you towards Sindi just as your past might some day drive you away from him."

"I don't agree with that," June said angrily. She was leaning on an elbow now and I could see the swell of her breasts! "What do you think?" she said looking at me. I didn't look into her eyes because I knew if I did, I'd lie. I had to tell the truth. This was perhaps the last chance.

I said Arun was right. I wanted to explain what I meant but I couldn't think of the right words. Karl had started shouting once more.

"Oh, you Indians!" he said throwing his arms in the air.

"You must all be half crazy. What do you think you are, a nation of saints or something?"

I wondered why he kept on generalising about Indians as if Arun and I constituted the entire Indian race.

I said it was difficult to be a saint if one didn't have any faith.

Karl replied vehemently that he for one had no faith and what was more he didn't feel the need for one.

"Nor are you a saint, my dear Karl," I said. "But what you said is not true. You have a faith in yourself as a free agent. I have lost even that."

I had not intended to talk about myself but it had just slipped out. The harm was done. June was already patting my knee. "Poor boy, poor boy," she said. "You need some sleep. Come here, I'll give you half my blanket."

After lunch Arun said he was going to comb the beach for sea shells. He said his landlady was crazy for them. Karl went along with him just to keep him company. June and I lay down to sleep. The ball players had broken up for lunch. The sea made the only sound as it flapped against the rocks like a restless bird. It was the kind of quietness that makes one look at oneself like an outsider. My eyes were two little slits of blue. Above me stood my soul like a bedraggled beachcomber that had searched the beaches of the world and found nothing. I saw myself as a child listening to the conversation of my uncle's friends. They had all treated me as a grown-up. "To love," my uncle had said once, "is to invite others to break your heart." My uncle was dead but the words lived on within me. The scene shifted to a flat in London. A woman, old enough to be my mother, crying in my arms. "I want you, Sindi, I want you, I want you. Please don't leave me." You said you wouldn't leave her. But she knew you would. And what was worse, you knew it, too. You leave her and many months later you find her dead drunk in a bar. At last you know what it is to break a heart. But the knowledge leaves you only puzzled. Fear of retaliation from an unknown power grips you. You have generated pain. To create pain is a crime. You can't get away with it. You try to build up your defences. You try to be careful, yet a part of you almost longs to be punished for the sin. It waits expectantly for the blow, and when it finally comes, it exults under the tearing pain. But the other half suffers in the bewildering agony. Suddenly you realise something has ended, something that you had heavily banked upon. Suddenly you want to cry, only you don't know how to go about it. Your face is distorted with uncontrolled pain that no amount of philosophy can ever rationalise. You bury your head in a pillow, hoping the blackness will bring tears but nothing happens. Uncle's words come back to you. You know what it is to love and have your heart broken. You grasp the essence of pain. What used to be an abstract idea now spreads through your blood like poison. It rages through the inner-most arteries

69

of your soul, corroding and destroying all that is tender in you. It swallows up all that you thought was most indestructible. The fire may last a week or it may last months, but it dies. It dies when there is nothing to feed on. And it leaves you dead, dead and immune and wiser. You sometimes think of God as you walk among the ashes of your dreams. Sometimes you build, again, sometimes you don't. But if you build, you build with wisdom. If you are lucky you put back into the world the wisdom the world taught you.

"What is the time?" June whispered sleepily.

"Three."

"We should be going back," she said, and then went back to sleep.

The blue slits closed and opened again. Time. The memories came flooding back. Time. A business executive reciting T. S. Eliot in a bar, his immaculate suit just a little wrinkled with the long sitting. Time. His sonorous chairman's voice above the din.

> *There will be time, there will be time.*
> *To prepare a face to meet the faces that you meet.*

And my reciting back at him:

> *And indeed there will be time*
> *To wonder, "Do I dare?" "Do I dare?"*
> *Time to turn back and descend the stair.*

Finally I slept. When I awoke I found a five-year old girl staring into my face. "The ball. Give me the ball please." Three of her front teeth were missing. I followed her gaze. A moist soft ball lay between June and me. "Give me a kiss first." Without hesitation the child knelt down, her wet mouth brushing against my cheek. Then she stood up, snatched the ball from my hand and was gone with a shriek.

June was awake and staring at me in a strange, half smiling, half puzzled, manner.

"You are funny, aren't you?" she said.

"I love little girls. You must have been like that when you were a child." I said, indicating the fleeing child.

It was only after we were halfway to Boston that I realised the full meaning of what I had said.

70

The northern lights hung low over Boston like an artist's dream. Karl and Arun got off at Washington Street. They said they wanted to go to the movies.

June asked me where I wanted to go.

"Home, I guess."

"I'll come with you."

I felt so tired and sleepy I lay down on the bed. June went into the bathroom. Then through the mist of euphoria I heard her in the kitchen, making coffee perhaps. Soon after I fell into sleep, one of those brief, depthless sleeps that you get when you are thoroughly exhausted.

When I woke up June was lying beside me. She had lain before in bed with me, but this was different. The very air seemed different. There was desire in the air. I instinctively knew what she wanted. We were near the brink; the end had come.

June was leaning over me. I stroked her hair and her cheeks. She smiled with half closed eyes. When she kissed me her mouth was warm, almost hot. It was different from the kisses she had given to the sick man; this time I was her lover. "Get up," a voice cried within me. I knew that was the last chance. Five more minutes and I would be involved up to my neck, bound hand and foot. But desire glued me to that bed. The contract had already been made. I slipped my hand under her dress. I felt her soft warm limbs and a flood of tenderness rose within me. It poured out of my finger tips and out over her young body. June got up and took off her dress. She still had the bikini on. Then she took that off, too. When she lay down in my arms again, her body shivered with passion. Desire rose within me like water behind a broken dam. I nearly cried with the burden of my lust. I had almost forgotten what a woman felt like. One had to begin again. One had to begin and wait patiently for the end. One could only hope that it was not painful.

For a long time after it was over, June lay still in my arms.

"I wanted to give you something for your birthday. This year has been different from the last. No?" she giggled.

A little later she turned her face towards me and snuggled in the crook of my arm.

"I think I love you," she whispered. "I don't know why."

"It is difficult to be saint," I said.

"What did you say?" she murmured sleepily.

"Nothing."

71

Then she fell asleep. I stayed awake, counting the broken pieces of my detachment. I counted the gains and the losses mocked me like an abominable joker. Then I, too, fell asleep.

8

THERE WAS the morning after the act. There were many mornings after the act. June always left at night; otherwise her mother would have got worried. I lived in a strange world of intense pleasure and almost equally intense pain. I say almost, because, had the pain been equal to the pleasure, I would have gone mad. At a later stage all pleasure drained out and only pain remained, but I shall come to that.

We met every day at first and then, on my suggestion, we cut it down to every other day. I was afraid I was running out of topics. Of course, June always had something new to say about what she did at the office, what she said to so-and-so and how she told her boss off when he made a pass at her.

I enjoyed listening to her and I liked her Boston accent. I enjoyed watching her eyes as they lit up with mirth or grew pensive at the thought of somebody's pain.

We used to meet after her office in a small cafe near the university, for a cup of coffee before going to my flat. The lady who owned the cafe had known me for three years and now she greeted me with pleasant amusement in her gentle, old eyes. Once she cornered me and whispered so that the whole cafe could hear, "you're gettin' to be a man now, a real man. An' such a nice lookin' kid, too." I laughed awkwardly. Luckily nobody was listening. When she got to know June better she started talking to her, too. She would serve us coffee and then chat for a minute or two. Once she said to her, "Hold on to him now. Slippery as an eel, that's what he is. One of these girls here once fell in love with him and I said to her, 'Take care honey, you might as well fall in love with a shadow. You can't love a stranger, now can you'?" June laughed it off but I could see that she had become thoughtful.

"This is the first time I have heard about it," I said laughing.

"I am not thinking of that," she said. "I am wondering whether you *can* love a stranger."

After coffee we usually went to my flat and cooked dinner. There were three large windows in the west wall of the kitchen. And when evening came, the sun rushed shouting into the house. It poured gold over our hands and on the peeled potatoes and in our eyes.

"Your eyes are like jewels when sunlight falls on them," she said once.

Karl worked late at the labs in those days and he ate outside. June and I split the work. I usually made salads and peeled potatoes; she cooked the meat. Sometimes we made love before dinner and it was beautiful to walk about later in the presence of warm, moaning passion. While I peeled potatoes, June would come up from behind and put her arms around my waist and press her cheek against my back.

"I love you," she would whisper, or "How your beard has grown since morning," or "You were wonderful today." She might have said anything and yet it would have meant the same. It meant that she wanted me and that was enough to feed my vanity.

Occasionally, we went to June's house and played antique gramophone records. There was an old three penny opera satirizing Nazi Germany which June liked very much. I didn't understand much of it but I enjoyed sitting there, looking at her father's portrait, wondering what sort of a man he might be. Mrs. Blyth made gorgeous dinners for us; she made marvellous garlic bread and I liked to stand around the oven inhaling the fragrance as if I were in an opium den. I wondered how much she knew about us. What would she say if she knew that I had been making love to her daughter only an hour ago in all her nakedness? Would she be angry?

"Have you told her about us?" I asked June once.

"No, not yet. Do you want me to?"

"I don't know. I suppose not. But I thought you told her everything."

June laughed a short little laugh. "Not everything," she said.

Many months later June told me the reason for not letting Mrs. Blyth in on the secret. She didn't like June having affairs, and certainly not with non-white foreigners. She would have thought I was making use of June and the pain would have been unbearable. June had planned to let her mother know if it came to anything.

73

On weekends we often went out of town. June had an old Chevrolet that seldom gave trouble but, when it did, it was out of commission for weeks. Usually, we went to the sea. Of course, it was too cold for bathing but we enjoyed standing on the beach with our arms around each other, watching the barren beauty of the grey landscape. It always tickled June when I turned my head and bit her ear. For some unknown reason, she said it reminded her of her childhood. On these occasions June always carried a basketful of eatables and a box camera. She took all kinds of pictures, like a bird sitting on a rock or I eating a sandwich or the sun going behind a tree. Later on she showed them to her mother. Most of these were quite ordinary, if not inane, but they seemed to enjoy looking at them.

When we had longer holidays, we drove out to the mountains of Maine and New Hampshire. We never did anything spectacular. We ate when we wanted to and made love when we felt like it. And after we had made love we usually ate again. In brief, we lived like animals when we went out on these holidays. I never did any thinking except when I was talking to June about some serious problems. At such times I was forced to think under an extraordinary compulsion to say nothing that I didn't, at the moment, consider to be the truth. I always prefaced my comments with. "This is what I believe at the moment," but I might as well have skipped it; it made very little difference.

Days went by like this. I became more fond of June with every passing day. Her thought would come to me while I was studying or putting instruments together or just crossing a road. At night when I went to bed I would find her fragrance on my pillow. Little things belonging to her lay scattered around the house. I would gather them and put them in a closet and a strange tenderness would grow within me. I allocated one drawer to her. I would fold her blouses and put them in her drawer and I would feel as if I was taking care of a deeply loved child. I would buy little presents for her because I knew how much she enjoyed presents from me even though they were of little value. I knew what food she liked and I bought it for her whenever she came home to eat. Sometimes, when I was supposed to see her but couldn't for some reason or another, I missed her.

And when autumn turned to winter and snow began to fall I discovered that whenever she was not with me I felt as if I had lost something. I even began to grow a little jealous when she talked admiringly of some other man. And at times I made love to her not because I desired her but because I wanted to make sure that she still loved me.

All this was only too familiar and it disturbed me. I knew I was getting involved. It had not happened to me for years and I had come to believe that it would never happen again. I thought I had conquered desire and the pain that it had brought me. But here I was pushed once again on the giant wheel, going round and round, waiting for the fall. There were others on the wheel who apparently never fell. But I didn't have 'heir luck. I wasn't born to ride the giant wheels of the world.

What made matters worse was the fact that nearly every time we met, June told me that she loved me. This only aggravated the burden of my guilt. Sometimes she asked me if I loved her. I told her I didn't know what she meant by that but I supposed I loved her as much as I loved myself. To this she would say that if that was the case I didn't seem to love myself very much. She said it lightly but that was more or less the truth.

I think she had hoped that as time went by I would come to love her more. I had already given her whatever I had and there was nothing more to give. Time could be of very little help. I tried to explain this to her once or twice but she always laughed it off, saying that I talked like a banker. I didn't quite see what a banker had to do with it, but I kept quiet.

Several times as we lay in bed June had suggested that we get married. She said we were both growing old and she wanted my children. It was the first time a woman had said she wanted my children. I felt like a bankrupt manufacturer who suddenly discovers that he has something to sell. I tried to imagine myself living in one of those inexpensive suburbs outside Boston, driving ten miles every day and going back to June and the children I had given her. The thought left me with no other feeling except that it seemed quite impossible. And, consequently, I didn't see any point in further elaborating it.

At times, she became sad, especially after making love to me. At such times she would say that her life had no purpose. I would ask her what she wanted to do in life. She said she didn't have any clear aims except that she wanted to be of use to someone. But these speculations were only a passing feeling with her and she soon recovered her usual gay self.

Nearly six months passed this way. I did well in my studies and I passed the preliminary exams for my Ph.D. with little difficulty. I still remember the long evening in my apartment when we celebrated my success while the winds brought the first big snow to Boston. But the winds of existence also brought Babu and our lives took a different turn.

9

THE FIRST time Babu met June was at my flat. He came up the stairs breathless, and when he saw us together he was thrown into confusion.

"I...I am sorry," he stammered, "I didn't know you were busy."

I could see from June's expression that his confusion was what she liked about him.

"I am not busy," I said. "This is June."

Babu stretched out his hand and blushed. He sat down in the chair self-consciously.

"Are you cold ?" June asked.

"Yes. This is my first snow."

"Haven't you ever seen snow before? What part of India are you from?"

"Delhi," he said and shivered visibly.

"You must be very cold," June said. "We will warm you up in a minute."

She walked up to him and started rubbing his hands between her own. Then she knelt down and opened his jacket. She put her mouth to his chest and began to blow into his sweater. It was all too swift for Babu to react in any way. But gradually, when he realised what was happening, panic spread over him. He couldn't push her away because to do that he would have had to hold her head. He couldn't even get up, because June had firmly clasped his hands. In utter bewilderment he looked at me beseechingly. I was in a fit of laughter.

It reminded me of the night we had got stuck in the woods, yet I couldn't help noticing the comic side of it. By the time I got around to doing anything, June had finished.

"There," she said buttoning up his jacket, "we must now get you an overcoat and a hot cup of coffee. Where is your overcoat, Sindi?"

She wrapped him up in the coat and then went to the kitchen to make some coffee.

"Well, are you feeling better?" I asked, in way of making conversation.

"Yes, much better. I think I caught a chill coming out of the subway."

"I don't suppose it ever snows in Delhi."

"No, never. You are an Indian, yet you are so terribly ignorant of India."

"I can't help it, you know. I have never been there."

We were silent for a while. Then he asked me in a whisper, "Who is June?"

His question amused me a little. I said she was a friend of mine.

"She is very pretty and all. Are you going to marry her?"

If I didn't ask him to mind his own business it was only because I was afraid of hurting him.

I told him we were just friends and I had no plans to marry her. For some reason, unknown to me, and perhaps unknown to him, he looked relieved to hear that.

"Do you mind if I made friends with her?"

I said I didn't mind what he did so long as he didn't drag me into it.

He lowered his voice still further and said,

"Do you think she will like me?"

I said I couldn't say as I didn't know what she thought of him.

Then to change the topic I asked him how his studies were going.

He said he was still getting used to the American system. He said it was so very different from what he had at home. "Here they give you a test almost everyday and they don't even tell you that they are going to do it. In India you have an exam once in two years and you don't have to worry until a few months before the finals."

I asked him if he had passed his tests so far. At this his face fell a little and he avoided my eyes. Then he said that of the five exams he had taken until then he had passed two. But, he added, he hadn't done too badly in the other three either and he hoped to make up the difference in subsequent tests.

77

I had a feeling he was fooling himself but I didn't say so; it was none of my business. We were silent for a while. June sang in the kitchen as she washed the coffee cups. Her singing mingled with the sound of running water and lilted through the house. It enveloped us like a lullaby heard in a dream and wove through our little separate worlds. She seemed to belong there more than the doorpost and the fireplace. The fireplace and the doorpost could go without making much difference but that shabby apartment without her singing would have seemed empty.

Suddenly Babu said, "Congratulations!"

"For what?"

"For passing your prelims. I read it in the college bulletin." I discerned a note of admiration in his voice.

I laughed and said thanks, "Are you going back to Kenya after your education and all?"

"I don't know. Probably not. I haven't thought of it yet."

June came in and sat down near me.

"Where else would you go?" Babu was always so curious about other people.

"I don't know. I may go to India. It is all the same." The topic was beginning to bore me.

"Why don't you stay on in America."

I said I was not made for America.

"What do you mean you are not made for America?" June said, almost in anger, I thought.

I grinned at her; she looked so pretty after her exertion. "It is much too sterilized for me. Much too clean and optimistic and empty."

"But you said it is all the same to you where you go," Babu said.

"It is all the same so long as I live among human beings," I said, deliberately taking the extreme stand. "America is a place for well-fed automatons rushing about in automatic cars. I'd go mad if I had to do that."

"I don't see why you are so against America," Babu said vehemently. "I think it is a wonderful country. I would never go back to India if I had the choice."

"Why don't you have the choice?" June said.

"My father would never agree to it," he said mournfully. "I'm an only son, you see," he added with a touch of pride and regret.

78

"Maybe a woman would change your mind," I said laughing. Babu blushed and shifted uncomfortably. "Would your father not let you stay on in America even if you married a girl here?" June asked.

"I don't think so. He'll be very angry if I married here."

"You must have a terrible sort of a father," June said mockingly.

Babu looked hurt. His eyes flitted between June and me, while he pondered what to say.

"He is not terrible," he said sullenly. "He is just orthodox. My sister is very modern. She has very progressive views on these things."

June asked him if his sister was also studying.

"She finished her M.A. last year. And do you know she broke the all India record in history."

June nodded her head, looking suitably impressed.

"What is she doing now?"

"She is helping my father in his business. And she is very clever and all."

Babu had this funny habit of saying "and all" after his sentences. After I got to India I discovered it was the way they teach them in some of those fancy schools.

"I am sure you love her," June said beaming.

"I absolutely adore her!" Babu replied with unnecessary emphasis.

I patted June's shoulder. "Your coffee is ready." I said to June when the crisp fragrance crept in from the kitchen. Babu stared at her back as she went out. Then he turned to me.

"I like her," he said in a confidential whisper. I kept quiet. I didn't know what he wanted me to say.

"She hardly knows me but even then she is so nice and all," he said.

He was about to say something else when June came in with the coffee and some doughnuts. She served us and then poured a cup for herself and perched on a chair like a model hostess. She asked Babu how long he had been in America.

"It will be two months next Monday," he replied.

"How do you like it?"

"I like the place. But I feel cold and lonely, especially at night."

"Haven't you made any friends yet?" I could already hear the note of pity in her voice.

"Not many. Of course, Sindi has been very helpful and I know a few other Indian boys. But I want to make American friends. I don't want to mix with Indians all the time."

"What is wrong with that?" June asked.

"You don't develop fully if you stick around only with your own countrymen."

I wondered whether it was his father or his progressive sister who had said that.

June said, "Americans have their own faults, you know. You may not find them very congenial towards foreigners."

"I like their dash." Babu said enthusiastically. "Indians are so underdeveloped as compared to them. Sometimes I wish I had been born in America. Not that I have anything against India but there is nothing to beat America."

For me the most confusing thing about Babu was the naivete with which he talked about his own feeling. But it was something that many people, especially June, liked about him. She explained to me many months later that this naivete in a large measure made and subsequently broke the bond of affection which grew between them.

We finished our coffee and doughnuts and then went for a drive in June's car because Babu had said he wanted to see the snow. June wanted me to drive. Babu insisted on sitting in the back seat. When we finally coaxed him to sit in the front he clung self-consciously to the door so he would not touch June. He still wore my overcoat and he looked like one of those dancing bears I had seen in pictures.

For some reason that drive has stuck in my memory. The roads were covered with ankle-deep snow and it was still falling in thick heavy flakes like a horde of parachuting angles. There were few cars on the road. June had put chains on the tyres and I felt as if I were driving a tank. We skirted the river and turned on to Riverside Drive. The river lay frozen and glazed like a blind man's eye, staring into the chaotic sky. Beyond it the lights of Boston seemed to belong to another world, the world of Christmas trees and gift stockings. It would soon be Christmas, I thought. My fifth Christmas on these alien shores. And yet all shores are alien when you don't belong anywhere. Twenty-fifth, Christmas on this planet, twenty-five years largely wasted in search of wrong things in wrong places. Twenty-five years gone in search of peace, and what did I have to show for achievement; a ten-stone body that had to be fed four times a day, twenty-eight times a week. This was the sum of a life-time of striving.

Inside the car all was quiet except for the monotonous hum of the heater. Babu had relaxed. June stared ahead solemnly. She was leaning slightly against me and I could feel the fullness of her thigh. Periodically she muttered something to herself. She seemed to have picked up that habit from her mother.

We were now on the main highway to New York. The pathlessness of the bone-white road was sad and beautiful. Huge trucks passed us periodically, looking like bright-eyed ghosts carrying their massive cargo to the skyscraper city. Other men like me waited there. Snow or no snow, they had to have their twenty-eight meals a week. Once we almost slid off the road.

"Shouldn't we go back?" Babu said. I thought he was scared a bit.

"Are you afraid I'll land you in a ditch?"

"Why should I be afraid?"

June said, "Let's have some coffee and then we'll go back."

We drove into a Howard Johnson. The place was deserted except for an old truck driver and a waitress. This was roadside America at midnight: bright, clear, and lonely as a heap of stainless steel. The brightness and the warmth revived Babu. He took out his hands from the overcoat pockets and started drumming idly on the table. The waitress ambled up leisurely to take our order. She was a plump little girl with pitch black hair and hands like two pink fish in the pockets of her waterproof apron.

"I would like some more doughnuts," Babu said to me in a whisper. He was like a child asking for sweets.

June asked him if they ate doughnuts in India.

"Only upper class Indians do."

"Why? Are they very expensive?"

"No. They are not expensive. But the lower class people are just not progressive."

While we drank our coffee, the truck driver got up and walked to the counter. He had a wrinkled old face and looked like Gary Cooper.

"Two tablets of No-Doze, please," he said.

He stared at us absent-mindedly as he swallowed the pills.

"It's going to be rough driving up to New York," he said staring out of the chromium plated doors.

"Why don't you wait till it's day?" the girl said.

"Can't. Boss will lose the contract. I've got a whole lot of Christmas goodies stuffed in there," he said tonelessly, waving towards the truck.

"Isn't it wonderful?" Babu was saying. "It's snowing outside and we sit here in this warm place eating doughnuts and all. Where else will you find this?"

"In hell and all," I said just to make fun of him. I was getting tired of his chatter.

"Why aren't you ever serious?" June said.

"I *am* serious." I said laughing.

"How is Daisy?" the girl asked.

"Fine, I guess," the truck driver said absent-mindedly. "I wish the snow would stop."

"Maybe it will. Wait an hour an' see."

"Can't. Got to hit New York by five."

"Don't they have such places in India?" June asked.

"No, not yet. I might make some when I get to be managing director of my company," Babu said.

"What do you manufacture?" I asked casually.

"Radios and heaters and home appliances. We would soon be making a lot more."

"You reckon this No-Doze stuff is any good?" the truck driver was saying.

"I guess so," the girl said. "Are you worried?"

I looked up at him. He did look rather worried. Somehow I had developed a strange, warm feeling for the man. I wanted to take his hand and tell him to hell with the Christmas goodies. New York could live without them. He said "I feel so sleepy. Haven't seen a bed for two days."

"Busy?" the girl asked in a sympathetic tone.

"Sort of. Daisy's friends keep dropping in for a drink. Christmas comin' up, you know."

"When is Christmas?" Babu asked.

"A week from tomorrow," June said.

"What does one do?"

"What do you do, Sindi?" June said.

"Nothing. Just sit around pretending I'm Santa Claus."

"Oh, Sindi," June said in mock exasperation.

"Reckon this snow ain't gonna stop," the man said with a sigh of resignation.

The girl didn't answer.

"I feel sleepy," said Babu, yawning.

"Do you think I should take two more pills?"

"I don't know. I guess you might." The girl said without looking at him.

The man swallowed his pills and put on his gloves. Hands of America were ready to steer Christmas over pathless roads. For a moment he paused under the porch looking up at the bloodless sky. Then he walked up to the truck, erect and confident, ready to deliver his goods. This was the America that the Statue of Liberty had forlornly presided over for decades. The truck roared to life. The search was on again, the search for wrong things in wrong places. The truck blinked its light and rolled onto the highway. There was not turning back now; no end to the fruitless search. The girl looked out absently into the white darkness, idly fingering the quarter left by the truck driver. Then she pressed the appropriate keys and the cash register clanged to mark the passage of a lonely traveller.

Somehow the whole thing had depressed me. There was something wrong about a man having to drive hundreds of miles in blinding snow when he hadn't seen a bed for two days. He probably made a lot of money in the process, but still it didn't seem right. While I thought this over, June and Babu discussed how Indian marriages were arranged. They had grown quite friendly in the short time that they had been together. June had a knack for making friends with people. Babu was saying how unusual a girl his sister was because she refused to accept an arranged marriage. This sister of his seemed to be a unique woman. I told this to Sheila when I saw her in India, but she merely burst into tears at the suggestion that her brother admired her.

When they had finished discussing the pros and cons of arranged marriages, Babu yawned loudly and said that he wanted to go home. I paid the check and we left.

We dropped Babu first. Then I drove to my apartment. On the way June said, "Babu is quite a sweet little boy, isn't he?"

I said I didn't know but I supposed he was.

"I like him," June said.

"He likes you too," I replied.

83

"Why are you both so different from each other?" she said, putting her head on my shoulder.

I said I did not see any reason why we should not be, considering the fact that we were two different individuals.

"What I meant was that since you are both Indians one would expect you to be fairly similar in many things. He doesn't even talk like you. You have such a nice British accent."

I said that was just a matter of what schools you went to.

She dropped me at my apartment. Just before leaving she said, "You *are* coming for Christmas, aren't you."

I said I'd try.

"If you don't I'll never talk to you again," she said pouting her lips.

I put my arm around her shoulders and kissed her on the mouth. "I'll come."

"I don't know what I'd do without you," she said looking up at me.

Suddenly I thought of Babu, I said.

"Why don't you call Babu, too. He would perhaps have nowhere to go."

"I will," June said. "Sometimes you are so nasty to him." Then she left.

For a long while after she was gone I stood on the pavement getting covered with snow. I get these moods sometimes and just stand around in the middle of the night when it is snowing or raining. It gives me a sense of aloneness and that is about the only way of feeling alone in these maniac cities. While standing there I began to wonder whether I had been nasty to Babu. If June said I was nasty she must have had a reason for it. Anyway, I thought, I'll make up to him when I meet him on Christmas Day.

And when Christmas came it was still snowing. I didn't have a hat or earmuffs and by the time I got to June's place my ears were aching like they had been sliced off. There was a big fire crackling and everybody crowded around it. Besides Babu there was a Japanese girl whom June had met in the subway. I sat beside her when I noticed that June and Babu seemed to be discussing something intimate. I didn't want to disturb them.

The little Japanese woman looked brilliant enough and she kept talking of a lot of subjects. But half the time I could not make out

84

what she was saying. She jumped from one subject to another, skipping her verbs and never finishing her sentences. Worst of all, she used words I had never heard of. She was describing how they celebrated Christmas in Japan. Then she switched to the American occupation of Okinawa. She seemed to be terribly excited about something but I really could not keep up with her speech. Consequently, I laughed when she laughed and looked serious when she became serious. I tried hard to concentrate. But every time I tried, my mind got off on a different trail.

June and Babu were sitting under the huge photograph of June's father, discussing serious things. Babu seemed much more at ease and I had a feeling he was enjoying being more or less alone with June. It had been a long time since I had gone to somebody's home for a Christmas dinner. For the preceding three years I had eaten my Christmas dinner in a cafeteria near Harvard Square along with old men in tattered overcoats and a sprinkling of Negro foreign students. I knew that most of them would again go there. The thought made me sad.

I had got out of the crowd because a girl had taken a fancy to me. It all seemed rather ordinary. I noticed that the little lady had stopped talking and was looking around awkwardly. We got up and joined June and Babu. Babu had drawn a crude map of India on a sheet of paper and was explaining the monsoons to her. June looked on frowningly, her forehead slightly wrinkled with concentration. I remembered that she had once asked me about the monsoons and I had put her off because the question bored me. She looked very pretty sitting there with her chin in her hand, her eyes sparkling with animation. She had on a blue dress that she had recently bought because I had said I liked it. It fitted her tightly around the hips and stretched out sensuously across the thighs. And I was her lover. She said she had had one before but that was experimental. I was *the* lover. For the time being I owned that blue dress and all that lay packed within. I owned that small head which constantly thought of me and wanted me and devised ways of making me happy. If I had suggested that I wanted her at the very moment she would have unquestioningly found means of giving herself to me in some quiet corner of the house. The burden of her love lay immensely on the debit side of my mind. And there were no credits. I had nothing to give her in return. I had given her what affection still remained with me. But that was not enough.

Sooner or later the balance would tip. June would ask for more but I would have nothing to give. That, I thought with a sigh, would be the end.

Babu now had an audience of two; the Japanese girl had joined them. I could see that she had already thrown in some incoherent questions which Babu and June were each interpreting differently.

"You see," Babu was saying "when they hit the Himalayas they *have* to turn west. There is no other way to go." He looked beseechingly at the little Japanese woman but she still looked unconvinced. Babu started once again. Like most of us, he talked very politely to foreigners.

I had not yet quite understood Babu. He was naive and a stuffed shirt and a snob and yet he was sensitive and affectionate. He may not have had the wisdom to discriminate between pain and happiness but he had enough affection to overcome somebody's pain, at least temporarily. He probably had received more love than I had and consequently had more to give.

During that evening Babu gazed at June with those dog-like eyes so full of adoration they embarrassed you. He was gay when June was gay and when she wasn't talking he became pensive. He watched her slightest desires and fell all over himself to meet them.

Later on in evening June tried to teach him to dance. Babu was so afraid of touching her he almost looked foolish. He blushed and refused to meet her eyes. When June insisted he should look at her and hold her closer he blushed profusely.

The Japanese girl asked me if I liked dancing. I took the hint and asked her if she would like to dance. We fumbled around the little room, following Frank Sinatra and occasionally stepping on each other's toes. The girl was a much better dancer than I, and I liked her perfume, but my thoughts kept flitting away. Babu had said he wanted to have affairs, by which he probably meant he wanted to have sexual experience. If he wants only that, I thought, he would get over it, but I had a feeling he was looking for something much more precious and devastating. Sex might have been the basis for his initial attraction towards June but it was rapidly changing to something else, something that would be much harder to get rid of. I had seen this happen before with some other foreign students and I was worried.

To divert my thoughts I looked at my young biochemist friend. She had full, sensual lips that she continually licked with a tiny pink tongue. Everything about her was tiny and precise except her speech.

"What are you thinking?" I asked, trying to make myself more agreeable.

"I don't think," she said.

"Never?"

"No. I don't think, now." She looked puzzled.

"I see," I said. "You dance very well. Where did you learn?"

"In Tokyo. My boy friend taught me. But I am not as good a dancer as June."

June's liquid voice rose above Sinatra's phoney racket as she and Babu went round the room: "one...two...three...one...two...three...once again. One...two... ." It reminded me of the little dancing school in Nairobi where I used to go when I was eight.

I don't remember whether it was after or before the dinner that we opened our stockings. I guess it was before dinner. Babu gave an unnatural yell as he pulled out one piece after another. He seemed to be getting a big kick out of the whole thing. I held on to my stocking self-consciously, feeling very awkward and foolish. Somehow I couldn't bring myself to slip my hand into that silly thing. I couldn't escape it, though with June watching me closely, I made a last attempt to get away.

"I'll take it home with me," I said to June.

"Oh, don't be a coward, Sindi. Come on now. It isn't going to bite you. Come now, come."

I pulled out a pair of studs, an expensive looking necktie and then, to my astonishment, a pipe.

"But I don't smoke a pipe," I said puzzled.

"I know," she giggled. "I want you to start smoking a pipe."

I said I didn't mind if she wanted it. I personally didn't care very much either way.

After everybody had looked over his goodies and everybody had thanked everybody else we went into the dinning room for dinner. I felt horrid for not having brought anything for June and Mrs. Blyth. I thought I'd do it the first thing the next day.

At dinner conversation inevitably veered round to India. June had just read Frank Moraes's biography of Nehru and she was all excited about him. Actually she was saying something pretty sensible, but in the middle of it Mrs. Blyth got off on her high horse and started doling out a lot of rubbish about her world trip. What the Indians needed, she said, was a better diet. I would have liked to ask her how

87

far the West had gone by gobbling up the millions of calories that it did. Of course, out of politeness I didn't. But she answered that, more or less, when she started comparing Americans and Indians.

"You wouldn't believe, June, how small they are," she said.

"About the size of sixth-grader. And they die at about thirty-two, don't they?" She looked at Babu for corroboration. Babu nodded without saying anything. I had a feeling Mrs. Blyth was hurting him just as she had hurt me the first day. Then she turned to me.

"Look what good diet has achieved in America," she said triumphantly like a magician.

I said, " I am sorry, Mrs. Blyth, but tell me where to look. What *has* good diet accomplished that could be called an achievement?" The little Japanese sniggered at this but Mrs. Blyth looked astonished as if I was asking a very foolish question! She hesitated for a minute. Then she said.

"We are taller with longer life and there is almost no disease to speak of."

"And what use have you made of your extra height and extra years? You carry heavier guns and have a longer time to make each other unhappy, that's all. Can you call that an achievement?"

"You are just a cynic, my boy," Mrs. Blyth said, patting my arm. "America wouldn't have been what it is today with your kind of cynicism."

I did not have anything to say to that; so we just let it go.

I finished eating and lit a cigarette.

June started gathering the dishes. Babu got up with alacrity to help her but he ended up by being in everybody's way. The Japanese girl went into the kitchen and brought back a tray full of strawberry cakes. One certainly didn't have a chance to find out what hunger was like with people like Mrs. Blyth looking after you.

After the cake and the cream we sat down around the fire sipping coffee. Suddenly I felt terribly sleepy. June and Babu had started talking about his studies. I thought Babu looked a little sheepish when he told her he was not doing very well. He said he was not used to so much homework and the popquizzes always caught him unawares.

"I know what you mean," June said laughing. "That's how I got flunked out of school."

"You mean you never graduated?"

"That is right," June said. For a moment Babu didn't know what to say. Then both of them laughed like children who have just heard a good joke. Babu was charming when he laughed. That was the difference between him and me. I could never have produced that laugh.

Then they started talking about some other crazy thing but I was so sleepy I couldn't keep track of what they were saying. The next thing I knew, they were talking about James Dean who had just died. After that they went into a complicated discussion of jazz and rock'n-roll. Now and then June tried to draw me into the conversation but when she saw that I was sleepy she let me be.

Mrs. Blyth had caught hold of the Japanese girl and I guessed she was really giving her the stuff on her world tour. Now and then the girl tried to interject but Mrs. Blyth went on uninterruptedly like a callous railway conductor.

Watching them, I dozed off. When I woke up the Japanese girl was sitting next to me. Mrs Blyth had disappeared into the kitchen. June was asking Babu what he did in the evening.

"Nothing much," Babu said. "Usually I try to study. But I feel so lonely I have started learning dancing." I wished he would stop talking about his loneliness.

"You are quite a bad dancer."

"I know, I need some practice," Babu said grinning and blushing at the same time.

Abruptly, June sprang to her feet. She put her hand behind Babu's neck and pulled him up.

"Come, let's dance some more. You do need some practice."

She put on some more records and they began to dance.

One...two...three.... One...two...three. It looked as if the counting would go on all night. I prepared myself for a long doze. But then the little Japanese woman leaned over and said something which shook me out of my stupor.

"Your friends seem to be very much in love with each other."

I was taken aback but I recovered quickly. I looked at my friends in a new light as they shuffled their feet in the far corner of the room, trying to strike a common pattern of dancing.

"You are very observant," I said.

"It is nice to see people in love," she said in a grand-motherly manner. "Are they engaged?"

89

"Not yet," I said. "Not yet."

I began to wonder what I would do if what the little woman said was true. I thought of a number of alternatives but finally I decided that there was very little that I could do. It was bound to happen sooner or later. If not Babu, it would have been someone else; it was bound to happen. One simply had to prepare as one prepared for death. In a way, it was like a small death.

June and Babu danced for another half hour before the party broke up. Then we all piled into June's car and plowed through the desert of snow like an army platoon in the Arctic. We dropped the little Japanese and Babu and then June and I went to my apartment. June asked me whether she could come upstairs with me for a while.

I was a bit sleepy but I told her to come up.

Once inside she became playful, like a little girl. She pulled my ears and poked me in the ribs, trying to make me laugh. She said I had been silent all evening and I must laugh now. Then she wanted me to smoke the pipe. I didn't particularly want to but I thought she would be hurt if I refused. Actually, it was a pretty good pipe and I liked it the moment I started drawing in the smoke. When I was puffing at the pipe, June slid down into my lap and put her arms around my neck. She had skin like velvet and I could feel the fullness of her body through the tight dress. She was gazing deep into my eyes.

"You look so solemn when you are smoking a pipe. I guess that is what I love about you—your solemnness."

She was clinging very close to me and I knew what she wanted me. Then she said, "Let's go into your room."

After it was over we lay still for a long time.
Then she said, "Darling?"

"Yes, my love?"

"It's time for me to go."

"There is no hurry."

"I don't ever want to go. I want always to stay with you." I had nothing to say, so I kept quiet.

June put her head on my shoulder and nestled against my neck. I kissed her hair and stared at the ceiling. A spider aimlessly walked upside down from one corner to another, exploring his inverted universe. Outside it was night and still snowing.

"Why don't we get married ?" June said suddenly. Her question surprised me with its abruptness.

"What do you want to marry a man like me for?"

She examined my arm, found a pimple and squeezed it out. "Stop putting on the modesty act," she said.

I laughed awkwardly. As a matter of fact I found myself rather tongue-tied. It had not been a modesty act. I had meant what I said. After a while I said,

"I mean what I said, June. I am not the right kind of man for you. Some people are not really cut out for marriage."

"And you are one of them?"

"Yes. I am afraid I don't really believe in marriage."

"I know you don't. You have said that before. But why. Sindi, *why*?" She seemed genuinely puzzled.

"Why? Why do some people believe in God and others don't? Can one ever answer that, June ? Can one ever explain one's beliefs?"

"But you must have some reason, honey."

Whenever June got a bit impatient she called me honey. It was like a twitch that came on automatically, like a warning signal.

I said that I might have had reasons to begin with, but now I was only aware of a dull fear. I was afraid of possessing anybody and I was afraid of being possessed, and marriage meant both.

"What is wrong with possessing or being possessed?"

I said there was nothing *wrong* with it. It was just too painful for some people and the point was whether one was built to take the pain or not. I didn't think I could, and that more or less settled the matter for me.

I put my hands on June's shoulders, she felt warm under the blankets.

"It is not that *all* marriages are painful. Here and there you run into odd-balls who know how to love without possessing. For the rest of them, it is one big illusion that has been pounded into them by society. For a while they go around bloated with their own pride imagining things which just are not there. And then gradually the whole thing crumbles and they begin to kill each other bit by bit."

"Oh, come now, Sindi. Surely everybody who marries is not sitting on a heap of crumbled illusions."

"Most of them, June. Only they do not have the eyes to see it. When they see this debris they get so confused that they walk into the first bar and get drunk or go to the Bahamas for a holiday."

"Well if others can live like that why do you have to be so sensitive?"

"It is not a matter of *having* to be sensitive, June. One is just made that way."

"One can also change. You don't always have to remain that way," June persisted.

I said she was right. One could change. But one must have a reason for changing. And I had none.

She looked at me for a long time. Then she said, "You would perhaps have one if you fell deeply in love with somebody."

"Perhaps," I said. I couldn't quite say what I would do if I fell deeply in love with somebody.

"You sound very doubtful."

"I am doubtful," I said laughing.

Then she asked me whether I had ever been in love.

I thought about my past and wondered whether my relationship with Anna or Kathy could be called love. Not by my definition anyway. I said,

"No. Not really."

Suddenly June became excited again. She pulled me down and snuggled against my shoulder. She said,

"I pity you. I pity my little brown Indian who has never been in love."

It had never struck me that one could be the object of pity because one had never been in love. And what did one mean by love anyway?

"How would you know when you have never been in love?"

"Perhaps I have. At least I have loved people as much as I love myself. It isn't much but that is not my fault. And then to be in love in your sense requires one to take things seriously, assume that there is a permanence about things. Nothing ever seems real to me, leave alone permanent. Nothing seems to be very important."

"Isn't it worthwhile to love somebody, make somebody happy, bring up children who contribute to society?" she asked.

"And then what? Death wipes out everything, for most of us anyway. All that is left is a big mocking zero." And besides, I wanted to add, I was worried about my own contribution, leaving aside that of my children.

92

June was quiet for a while. The spider lost hold of ceiling, hit the radiator and fell on the floor.

"In that sense nothing is important," she said dreamily, her voice acquiring the far-off quality that it did when she was thinking.

"That is precisely it."

"But that doesn't make sense," June said, her pretty forehead wrinkling a bit.

"You are lucky. The moment it begins to make sense you are lost."

"But you don't seem to be lost."

"I am, and I am not. I am lost in the usual sense of the word. And yet." I hesitated. I had never talked to anyone like this. "Good things and bad things appear to be the same in the long run of existence.

"But aren't you ruffled by the day-to-day happenings?"

"Not really. Things seem to even out."

"Would you be ruffled if I went away?"

I said I didn't know but most likely I wouldn't.

"I hate you," she said. Then she kissed me on the mouth and got up.

I watched her dress. She had nice skin, smooth and pink. Would I be ruffled if she went away? She hummed an old tune as she put on her clothes. Then she sat in front of the dressing table combing her hair. It fell in rich heavy curls around her long neck. Would I miss her if she went away? Our eyes met in the mirror. The burning blue seemed to pierce the opaque glass. She smiled softly at me and a strange sadness grew in the pit of my belly. My eyes grew misty. I got up and grasped her shoulders. I clung to her with an unusual fierceness and pressed my lips against her neck.

"Oh, my darling," I whispered, "You don't know how much I love you."

She looked at me with faint astonishment. Then she got up and put her arm around me.

"You never called me darling before," she said. "Kiss me." She was crying. And then she left.

I saw her come out of the house and turn into main street. Her hair shimmered as she passed under a street lamp. Would I be ruffled if she went away? I had to answer the question some day.

10

ONE DAY a few weeks after Christmas while I was working at the labs, Babu rang me up.

"Can you come and see me at once?" He sounded hoarse.

"What's the matter?"

"I can't tell you on the phone. Please come and see me," he pleaded.

"All right."

His room was a spectacle. Beer cans lay all over the place like fallen soldiers. Babu sat amidst these in his night gown, his eyes swollen.

"What's the matter?" I asked.

He looked at me and started crying.

"I have failed all my exams," he said sobbing.

"All of them?" I was surprised. Babu nodded, his face distorted with crying.

I did not know what to do or what was expected of me. I very much wanted to help Babu but I did not know how to go about it.

"How did it happen?"

"I don't know. I went up to see the results yesterday, least expecting it. And there it was. I didn't pass a single course."

"Not even drawing?"

"Not even drawing," Babu said. He wiped tears from his eyes.

"Hadn't you prepared well enough?"

"I had. For a whole week I hardly slept for four hours. I am not used to the type of question papers they set here."

After a while, with a sudden burst of anguish, he went on. "But I had answered most of them. I don't know what went wrong. I just don't know. Somebody might have a grudge against me."

"Oh, come on Babu, nobody has a grudge against you. Everybody fails once in a while. There is nothing wrong with it. It is especially difficult when you are not used to the system. I have seen a lot of foreign students have the same trouble."

"Did you ever fail?"

"No." I said reluctantly.

"Then why must I fail? Why must I?" He punctuated the question by hitting the wall with his clenched fist.

"I was pretty much near failing myself in the first term," I lied. "But you never actually failed while I *have*. How would I ever show my face again to the professors?"

"Have you seen the dean?"

"No, not yet. I came back straight home and started drinking. I just got up with an awful headache. I will be so ashamed to go and see him."

"You will have to, sooner or later."

"I know. Would they throw me out?" His voice was getting shaky again.

"No," I said. And yet I knew they might. They had done that in the past. Perhaps Babu learnt my thoughts.

"Are you sure they wouldn't ask me to go?"

"They probably wouldn't," I said more in the way of assuring myself than assuring him.

"My God," Babu said covering his face with his hands.

"What would father say when he comes to know about all this?" And he started crying again.

Something which absolutely unnerves me is the sight of someone crying. I strode up to Babu and clamped my hands on his shoulders. I shook him lightly.

"Don't get upset, Babu," I said. "Everything will work out. Let me go and see the dean and then you can cable your father."

Babu put his head on my shoulder and started crying in real earnest. He kept on worrying about what his father would say. "They would all be ashamed of me. My God, they would all be so ashamed of me," he kept on saying.

Half an hour later I went to see the dean. I had been one of his good students and I hoped he would listen to me. I had never asked a favour from anyone yet and I felt slightly awkward waiting in the lobby.

"Hullo, Sindi. How have you been?" The dean asked congenially.

"Fine, sir. I've come to see you regarding a friend of mine, Babu Khemka."

The dean clicked his tongue and shook his head.

"That boy hasn't done too well, has he? I don't know what's the matter with him. He's always there in the class and yet he seems to be constantly thinking of something else. He failed in all courses, didn't he?"

"He did," I said. "Are you going to ask him to leave?"

"I am afraid we will have to. Of course, the final decision is up to the committee."

I didn't know where to begin. Then I took the straight path.

"Please do me a favour, sir," I said earnestly. "Give him another chance."

The dean looked surprised. "But you know how badly he has done!"

"I know. But you don't know what state of mind he is in. I'm afraid he might do something drastic if you throw him out right now. I'm sure he will do better next time. It takes time for many of us to get used to the system here."

"I am not so sure he'll do better next time, but if you say so, I am prepared to reconsider his case. Let me look at his grades again."

Fifteen minutes later I came out of the dean's office with a tentative promise that he would give Babu another chance.

I called Babu and told him he needn't worry and that I would be seeing him in the evening. Then I went back to the labs and tried to work. But my thoughts kept going back to Babu. His crying had shaken me up. I tried to brush it aside as none of my business but I couldn't help imagining how lonely and miserable he must have felt. Angrily I wished he was not so damned afraid of his father and that he had not got me involved. The day passed.

In the evening, as usual, June and I had coffee together. The first thing she said was, "You look worried."

"Not really," I said. But then I told her about Babu.

"Poor boy, poor Babu," she said when I finished. "Are you going to see him?"

"Yes, I am seeing him this evening."

"Can I come along?"

"Yes, why not?" I said.

Babu was surprised to see both of us. He looked from one to the other, almost as if he expected us to have designs on him, but he relaxed when June smiled at him. He had dressed and cleaned up the room. He looked sad and handsome.

June and I took him to a very expensive restaurant on Park Street for no other reason except the delusion that the more expensive a dinner the more pleasurable it might be. But what June achieved in those two hours I couldn't have managed in two years.

96

June was one of those rare persons who have a capacity to forget themselves in somebody's trouble. I don't know how they manage it but it is beautiful to run into them every now and then. June perhaps was essentially so uncomplicated a person that whenever she saw somebody in pain she went straight out to pet him rather than analysing it a million times like the rest of us. And this is what she did that evening. She talked to Babu on whatever he wanted to talk about and told him what he wanted to hear. I was surprised at some of the lies she told, but in her scheme of things the lies were justified because they made Babu happy. I was silent most of the time but I enjoyed their conversation. It was wonderful to see Babu gradually come out of his shell and start smiling again. They talked of all sorts of things, ranging from June's exploits in school to snake charmers in India. Then Babu started talking about his family. On the one hand he loved his father, on the other he was mortally afraid of him. It didn't make sense to me then, but knowing Mr. Khemka personally it has begun to make a lot of sense now. Mr. Khemka, I suppose, is one of those fastidious persons who are so often found among big people. He was clever and successful and he seemed to expect everybody else, especially those whom he loved, to be clever and successful. And if they failed he became so emotionally involved that he destroyed what little capability they had. That, I suppose, had happened to Babu, although none of us realised it then.

During the course of the evening June asked him why he was so afraid of his father. For a moment Babu nearly clammed up. Finally he said he was not at all afraid of his father; it was just that he had a deep respect for him. What struck me as unusual was that he really believed it. Then he started talking about his sister, as he always did when somebody asked him about his father. He talked much more freely about his sister. Apparently he had great love and admiration for her. June asked him if his sister would be disappointed if he married a foreigner.

"No," Babu said. "She is very broad-minded and all." He said this as if he were telling us she was broad-hipped or had broad shoulders. The thought made me giggle.

"What are you chuckling about?" June asked. She hit my leg with her foot.

"Nothing," I said.

She turned towards Babu.

"Don't you think Sindi is sort of strange?"

Babu nodded his agreement.

"That is what I like about him, though," she said.

Suddenly lights in the restaurant became dim and the band started to play. One by one couples moved onto the floor. Under the table June entwined her feet with mine. She looked prettier in the low light. I wanted to ask her to dance with me, but I was afraid Babu would be hurt at being left alone. I was still wondering about it when Babu said to her, "Let's dance."

June agreed, it seemed to me, too eagerly. Babu had improved and I could not help admiring the ease with which he danced. They certainly presented a much better sight than June and I would have. Physically they seemed to be made for each other. Babu was tall and June could look up into his face. Occasionally girls turned around to look at him; they must have been struck by his dark good looks.

As I sat watching them I remembered what the Japanese girl had said. I too had a feeling that Babu was falling in love with her. The thought disturbed me, not because I was afraid of losing June—I still had sense to see that I must lose her some day although I hadn't quite imagined how painful it would be—but knowing June in a vague, intuitive way I was afraid for Babu. I had a feeling that Babu would not get from June what he wanted, and the realisation would come so late that he would be helpless to do anything about it.

When they came back June asked me to dance with her. But the mood had gone and I refused. Between courses, Babu and June danced some more.

"Come on, now, be a good boy. Come and dance with me," June insisted again. I thought she would be hurt if I didn't.

As we danced she clung to me with a somewhat unusual tenacity.

"Are you angry with me, Sindi?" she said, her mouth trembling a little.

"No, why should I be angry?"

"Why didn't you dance with me?"

"You know I don't like dancing. And then you were too busy dancing with Babu."

"You know that is not true." I noticed that her eyes were wet.

"Don't be silly, my love," I said.

"I hate you," June said, and laughed as suddenly as she had started crying.

98

After dinner, June dropped us at my flat and went home; she was expecting an aunt. Karl was asleep. I made some tea and we sat down in the kitchen. Babu cleared his throat and I winced inwardly.

"I must thank you, you know, for getting me off the hook."

I had nothing to say, so I concentrated on squeezing the last drop of tea out of the tea bag.

"My father would have ordered me to come back at once."

That would have been best for him, I wanted to say, but it would have been too demoralising, and then I was not quite sure of it.

"Well, you'll have to work very hard this time. You are supposed to make up for the first term as well." I felt very awkward talking like that but there was nothing else to say.

"Do you think I'll pass this time?" Babu said looking rather worried.

"I don't see any reason why you shouldn't."

"But I can't concentrate. I just can't concentrate. I sit down to read and go on flipping pages but my mind is elsewhere."

I asked him what happened in his mind.

"I think of home and Sheila and cars and some friends in Delhi and so on."

"What does the 'so on' include?"

He didn't reply immediately.

"Women, for example?" I prodded.

"Yes, women, I'm afraid I think a lot about women, Sindi." He was silent again. Then he added, "I know that I have come to finish my degree and everything must wait until I do so, but I just can't control myself."

"Why don't you get married?" I had said it in fun but Babu took it up seriously.

"I have thought of it myself," he said pensively.

"Don't you want to just play around anymore?"

"I'm beginning to change my mind," he said grinning.

"Why don't you find yourself a girl then," I said getting up and putting some more water on the stove.

"I would. But I am worried about my father. He will be absolutely furious."

"What is the worst he can do?"

"He would tell me never to show my face again. That would be terrible."

"Is that what's bothering you?" I laughed.

"You don't understand," he said. "You have never had a family." It came as just a plain statement of fact.

"Yes, I suppose you are right," I said, pouring another cup of tea.

Babu went on. "Whatever he may be, he has done a lot for me. He sent me here and I promised him I'll never marry in America."

"Too bad for you."

"Why are you always so sarcastic with me?" Babu said looking up, his dark eyes flashing with anger and self-pity.

I ignored his remark. I said,

"Would he not change his mind if he got convinced that you were marrying the right kind of girl?"

"But he doesn't think any American girl can be of the right kind," Babu said sulkily.

"Perhaps you can tell him that you can't pass your exams without getting married."

"That wouldn't do. He'll just ask me to come home and get married."

He had apparently thought about the problem in great detail. It made me suspicious.

"Well, that should serve your purpose," I said in order to confirm my suspicion.

"But I don't want to do that. I want to marry here." Then he got a bit confused and started to drink his tea that had been left untouched so far.

I got up and lit a cigarette. So he was already thinking of marrying June. He certainly made his decisions quickly, and it didn't strike him that I came into the picture in any way. He had never had to think of others when he wanted something.

"Listen, Babu," I said, "don't do anything in a hurry. Women are desirable creatures but they can also hurt you. We all make use of each other even though we don't want to. In your part of the world you marry only once in a lifetime. It is quite a serious matter. Don't just rush into a wrong thing for a temporary need."

Why was I saying all this? I was of course worried that Babu might make a mess of things if he was not careful. But beyond that it struck me that I was suddenly afraid. I was afraid of losing June.

"Don't worry, Sindi," Babu said getting up. "I'll take care of myself. I should be going home now. Would you please call a cab for me?"

After Babu was gone I had some more tea. For the first time in many years I found myself thinking of the future. I wondered how it was going to turn out. Once it would have turned out in just one way, but now it was pregnant with alternatives. And the choices I made now would inevitably lead me to one of the alternatives. And there was no getting away from what I had chosen so far. After years of struggle I had almost achieved what I had always wanted to be; without desire. But I had bartered away the gains in an attempt to possess a woman. I had exchanged the steady tranquillity of my being for the excruciating moments of ecstasy in a woman's body.

There was no getting away from all this. No going back. There was nothing to be done but wait. Wait and wait and let the past determine the future. I had lost much in an effort to gain what I could never have. In the quiet of that night, sitting in that shabby kitchen, I realised that now I should stay still. But the eternal joker snickered within me.

During the next few weeks I had to go to New York in connection with my project. I had a busy time there, working all day and sometimes at night. Occasionally, I went off by myself to one of the high points and watched the changing moods of the Hudson. On these occasions my thoughts invariably drifted to Boston and to June. I wondered what she might be doing. I wondered as if she and Babu were going out together, now that I was not there.

Once I got a letter from June. The sight of it made my pulse quicken. So long as she didn't write I could imagine anything I wanted. But a letter put things in black and white. A letter could put an end to everything.

"I miss you, darling." she began. "The weather is changing here and I think of the last spring when we first met." I could almost have cried on that. She talked a little bit more about ourselves; then she wrote "I have been seeing Babu frequently since you left. He seems to be in such low spirits most of the time that my heart aches for him. He is usually depressed because he is not doing well in his studies. I go out with him every night because I think he needs me. I want to be of use to him. Perhaps, as you would say, it is all an illusion: one can never be of use to anyone. Perhaps I am being selfish. All I know is that I find a strange peace when I am soothing him. I do so much want to be of help to someone, Sindi. Without that life would seem so empty."

The letter ended with a bit more about the weather and a comment about a new dress she had bought.

Was that the way the switch began? I felt like the pointsman who realizes with dismay that he has put the train on the wrong track and there is nothing that he can do about it. I wondered if she had already slept with Babu. The thought made me sick in the stomach. Then I tried to rationalise it. It is just because I am not there, I assured myself. And what if June has left me? I would speculate. Was I not supposed to remain detached under the circumstances? But I also knew that the more detached I became, the farther June would move away from me. Then I would go round in circles and start wondering once again whether I was going to lose her completely.

I tried to speculate about these things objectively, not realising that objectivity was just another form of vanity. I tried to imagine the worst and then persuaded myself that it could really not happen. Underlying all this was an assumption that June would not leave me, not for Babu anyway. What would she find in Babu that I didn't have? That was where I went wrong.

About a month later, I finished my work in New York and returned to Boston. The person I worked for apparently liked me and, just before I left, offered me a job in his department. I said I'd think it over. I had already been offered a job in Boston which seemed to be more meaningful and I wanted to stay on in Boston. But that was not the only reason for my wanting to stay in Boston.

It was a beautiful evening as I drove down from the Logan Airport. I hadn't been on that side since Babu came: he had been the last of the foreign students. The cab driver whistled a dainty tune as he sped down the tree-lined roads. I gazed wistfully at the landscape and the dusky sky. It was one of those evenings that make you feel you are lucky to be young. I was aware of a dull, pleasant ache in my limbs, a gentle throbbing of the muscles. I looked at my hands and moved my fingers. The blood rose under the pink nails and then disappeared, asserting the fact that I was alive. My thighs felt taut and warm. It was beautiful and I was glad to be alive.

As soon as I got to my apartment, I called June. Her mother answered. June had gone out, she said. "Has she gone out alone?" I asked, "No," Mrs. Blyth said, "she went with Babu." I wanted to hang up but she chattered on. She wanted me to come for dinner and tell her all about New York. I said I might.

I didn't want to go and talk to her about New York. I took a frozen dinner from the refrigerator and put it in the oven. It had Batch No. 39775 marked on it. Idly I wondered where the other dinners of the Batch No. 39775 could be.

It was warm inside the apartment and I decided to take a shower. I had an eerie feeling of floating in the air as the tepid water poured down my back. My mind flitted from object to object, in space and in time, and then came to rest upon June. I had thought of her all the way from New York and I had so much wanted to see her. I wondered where they had gone. Perhaps I should ring up Babu's flat. His landlady could probably tell me where they had gone. I might locate them, but what was the point? Did it really matter if I didn't see her for a day or if I never saw her again? I knew it didn't, and yet I also knew that things had suddenly seemed empty after that conversation with Mrs. Blyth. Spring blew in through the bathroom window and tickled my limbs. And then it struck me that there was still a chance of seeing June if I went along to Mrs. Blyth's for dinner.

The kitchen smelt of burnt gravy. Apparently, the oven had been too hot for Batch No. 39775. But the chicken was still preserved. I rolled it up in a piece of tin-foil and took it along with me.

Mrs. Blyth seemed more jubilant than usual. "Isn't it glorious weather?" she squealed as soon as she saw me. "It is," I said.

Strangely, her gaiety only had a dampening effect on my spirits. I shared my chicken with her and told her all about New York, adding little spicy titbits of my own to make it sound like a John Gunther inside. And all the time I was waiting for the ring of the bell, the familiar groan of the door and June's rapid footsteps. The clock struck ten and the little radio in the kitchen came up with its hourly bulletin of what passed for news.

"Does June stay out pretty late these days?" I asked.

"They have been going out almost every night for the last two months," Mrs. Blyth said, not without a hint of pride. Then she added.

"Babu is quite a boy, isn't he?"

I nodded. That's precisely what he was, quite a boy.

"And they go to such fancy places, I can't even pronounce their names. It must cost him a fortune."

"He is very rich," I said.

"Is he? Is he a maharaja?"

"Of sorts. He is a modern maharaja who makes electric kettles."

"How interesting," Mrs. Blyth exclaimed absent-mindedly. She was obviously thinking of something else. Another hour passed and the deep sonorous voice came once again on the air. The spring, it said, was expected to last four more days, it reminded me of a Swahili song which had a refrain: "Make love, dear friend, hold on to her thigh; For spring is a two-day wonder and tomorrow you die."

I was tired with the strain of waiting. I wasn't sleepy but I wanted to go to sleep, just to stop thinking about June. I thanked Mrs. Blyth for the pleasant evening and left.

"Come again," she called after me.

I walked all the way back to my flat. Mrs. Blyth was right; it was glorious weather. Amidst the hideous loneliness of those stone buildings it was the only thing that could give the city a claim to glory.

My apartment was warm and dark and quiet. Karl had been there while I was away. He had left a note behind saying that he would be away for the night—on business. I went into his room. It was in a chaotic state. Photos of pin-up girls hung limpy on the wall, attracting little more attention than cobwebs. The bed had not been made for ages. On the floor his antique record player lay open like a dead man's jaw, swallowing dust. A pile of records lay on the turntable, forlornly marking the end of a musical orgy. I pressed the button and suddenly the cavernous jaw came alive—everything moved, the turntable moved, the arm moved, the needle moved. Melodious packages of sound swung out of the cavern, floated out of the window and died. It was Vivaldi's "Seasons." That is what Kathy used to play every morning with tea that summer we spent together in Wales while her husband was away. With the dying seasons, Kathy too swung out of the window and died. I switched off the past and lay down to sleep. Just before sleep, once again I thought of June, but in a calmly detached manner. My tranquillity had returned. I had loved Kathy with a piercing, all-caressing love of an adolescent, and it had shattered the very roots of my existence when she went back to her husband; yet I had got over that. What did it matter if I lost June now?

I must have gone to sleep at once because half an hour later when the bell started ringing I shuddered with difficulty from the depths of a calm, luxurious stupor. I tried to go back to sleep but the ringing persisted. Swearing, I got up and flung open the door. I was a trifle surprised to find June standing on the landing.

"Hullo!" I said. "I didn't expect you."

"I know. I just came back and mother told me you had been waiting for me."

"Yes, I was, in a way. Has Babu come with you?"

"No. I dropped him at his house before going home."

We went into the living room and sat near the open window. The night had cooled.

"When did you come back?" she said.

"This evening. How is Babu doing?"

She was silent for some time. I scrutinised her face trying to understand what went on in her mind. She looked worried.

"Rather badly, I am afraid," she said at last.

"In what way?"

"In almost every way. He seems to have got into a vicious circle. He is doing badly in studies, and worse, he wants to let himself out in other ways. He thinks he'll come back to his studies with renewed vigour if he does a whole lot of other things."

"Does he really believe that?"

"He seems to, most of the time anyway," she said with a shrug. "But he gets very worried at other times, especially when he gets a letter from home. This father of his seems to be an awful bully. I am sure things would be much simpler if he were not always there in the background, sending those long sermons and telling him what's wrong with him and how he should carry himself."

"That is the price of love all sons have to pay."

"Aren't you glad you never had a father?"

"Perhaps I am. But I only know what it is not to have a father; I don't know how it would have been if I had one."

Unexpectedly, she laughed at this. I was still very sleepy but I couldn't help smiling. For a long while she stared at the window. She seemed to be turning something over in her mind.

"Babu is becoming awfully dependent on me, I am afraid," she said at last. Her voice trembled a little and she struggled to keep it matter-of-fact.

I kept quiet.

"Why don't you say something?" she said after a while.

"I have nothing particular to say. He is looking for friends and I am sure he likes you. I would not be surprised if he is very much in love with you."

"I am afraid of that myself."

"What is there to be afraid of?"

"It is just the kind of fear I used to have before taking an exam or jumping from the diving board. You never know whether you'll make it or not. Do you see what I mean?"

"I suppose I do. But what are you afraid of failing in this case?"

"Babu has begun to expect so much of me, so much more than I can possibly give him. I don't know where it is going to lead."

"Why don't you tell him?"

"Tell him what?" she asked looking up.

"Tell him that you can't give him all that he expects."

She laughed. "I wish I could do it but it's not as simple as that. I can't tell him, 'Look, Babu, I simply have run out of gas. You better look around elsewhere'."

"Why can't you do it?"

"I have a feeling it would hurt him terribly. Sensitive as he is, he would think I am trying to get rid of him, which I am not. And then perhaps I am too vain to tell him that I haven't got what it takes to be useful to another human being."

A gust of wind blew in through the window, ruffling her hair. A strand slipped from its fixed position and fell across her forehead. With a sudden pang I realised how beautiful she was.

"Tell me what to do, Sindi." Her voice was a soft husky whisper.

"You are your own master, little girl. And you are beautiful. Beautiful girls can do almost anything they like."

She moved across the sofa and put her hand inside my shirt. She felt my ribs one by one, like a mother or a nurse.

"How thin you have grown," she whispered. She put her arm around my neck and pressed her full mouth against mine. Her mouth opened under the caress of my tongue and I could feel the warm blood rising. Desire rose within me. I wound my arms around her waist and pressed her into me until she almost gasped for breath.

"I want you," I said.

She said nothing but got up and went into the bedroom. She had been sunning herself and her tanned body was lovely as a rose in the dim light. We made love with a strange fierceness that was as

106

excruciating in its pleasure as it was painful. And then just after the final moment her body was thrown into a paroxysm. She shuddered under me in a convulsion. She bit into my shoulder until blood came out and then I discovered that she was crying. I put my arms around her and tried to calm her down. She bit her lip and hid her face in the pillow. Then something seemed to break within her and she burst into uncontrollable sobs.

"It is all so meaningless, Sindi, so utterly meaningless. All we do is get into bed and... ." Her sobs choked her off.

I patted her hair mechanically. She was right, dreadfully right. After some time her body ceased to shake and she wiped her tears.

"Let's get married, Sindi. For God's sake, let's get married. I am so scared we might break up and all that we have would be lost."

I could feel the fear vibrating in her voice. The fear of loneliness; the fear of having to start once again. It almost caught hold of me, too. Yet, I knew that I must stick to the truth. Any lie, however well intended, could only be a time bomb with a fuse set for some time in the unknown future.

I said, "Marriage wouldn't help, June. We are alone, both you and I. That is the problem. And our aloneness must be resolved from within. You can't send two persons through a ceremony and expect that their aloneness will disappear."

"But everybody else gets married. Are they all fools."

"They are not fools. But they have the benefit of their delusions. Their delusions protect them from the lonely meaninglessness of their lives. It is different with me. I have no delusions to bank upon. I can't marry you because I am incapable of doing so. It would be like going deliberately mad. It is inevitable that our delusions will break us up sooner or later."

"Nothing is inevitable," June said vehemently. The edge of despair was breaking through her tears.

I was silent for a while, wondering what to say. Then I said what came straight to my mind. My voice sounded immensely sad even to my own ears.

"I am happy you look at the world that way, June. America has given that to you. The Statue of Liberty promises you this optimism. But in my world there are no statues of liberty. In my world many things are inevitable and what's more, most of them are sad and painful. I can't come to your world. I have no escape, June. I just have no escape."

"But don't you love me just a little, just enough to start with?"

Tears welled up in her eyes again. I continued in the same dirge-like voice.

"My darling, my beautiful darling, you have no idea how much I love you. But I have loved you in my own way. I know no other way."

I went on talking incoherently, and whatever came to my mind I formed into words. I tried to tell her how one becomes, what his memories make of him and at any one point in time the future is as inevitable for him as night follows day. It could be clear or it could be cloudy, or it could be torn in two by a storm, yet it is night. And even a thousand neons cannot neutralise its blackness.

June cried silently. I don't think she was listening. After a little while she dozed off, perhaps out of exhaustion. She was so much like a child. I looked at her calm, tear-drenched face and I found that I could not stop talking. I don't recall all that I poured out that night over that sleeping figure. I don't think it made much sense. And as I talked I kissed her, not from desire but just to find an outlet for my tenderness.

After about half an hour she woke up with a start and looked at her watch.

"My god, it is already two. Mother must be getting the jitters."

She jumped out of bed and dressed hurriedly. Then she sat before the mirror making her face up.

"How my eyes are swollen? And it is all because of you. Do you think mother will notice?"

"She'll probably be asleep when you get there." She got up, gave me a hurried kiss and rushed down the stairs. I heard the whine of the starter and suddenly I recalled the night in the woods. The roar of her engine died round the corner and I had a sickening feeling that she wouldn't want me anymore.

The next day spring burst upon Boston in all its splendour.

People discarded overcoats and students went about in highnecked pullovers. A dozen signs went up on Massachusetts Avenue announcing spring sales. Even the advertising jingles were revamped overnight. The river had thawed and was flowing once again. A yacht or two had appeared on the surface like stray swallows. Teenaged boys waited in front of theatres chewing gum, their hair glossy with cream. Numerous balls were announced simultaneously by the horde of associations, fraternities, social clubs, and I had been requested by the International Students Association to be one of the judges in their dance contest. Everybody wanted you to be gay and happy. Whatever griefs you may have had in your private universe, spring in America ruthlessly extracted its toll of gaiety.

The painful experience of that night weighed heavily on my heart. I had never seen anybody cry as I saw June cry that night. I rang her up a number of times but she was always out—usually with Babu. Each time Mrs. Blyth told me that they had gone out together, I sat down wondering whether June had really left me. Or, was she just trying to help Babu over another crisis? Strangely enough, I had ceased to hear anything from Babu. Once or twice I had run into him in the library but each time he had appeared to be in an awkward hurry to get away. At last one evening I got June on the phone. I asked her if she would like to go with me to the International Students Ball. I wondered if she remembered that it was at a similar ball a year ago that we had first met. She said she would have liked to but she had already promised to go with Babu. I said I was sorry about that last night we spent together. She said there was nothing to be sorry about. She saw my point and although she would have liked to follow me through the rest of her life, there was nothing to be done because I didn't seem to want her.

"That is not true, June," I said, for the first time feeling the sting of her anger.

"Perhaps not. But it amounts to the same thing."

"Yes, it amounts to the same thing," I said.

After this we hung up. It was obvious that I had lost June, yet such is the perverse nature of hope that I continued to delude myself with the feeling that it was all a temporary phase and that sooner or later she would come back to me.

I had a considerable amount of work to finish at the laboratory but I found myself unable to apply myself. Howsoever I tried, I couldn't stop thinking of June. Sometimes I thought of her objectively, trying to analyse the whole thing logically. At such times everything fell beautifully together and I came to the conclusion that what had happened to me was not only plausible but inevitable.

Babu had given her all she needed. She could be of use to him and he loved her with a dog-like devotion. Above all, he needed her. That was a trump that June could not resist. I had only the clubs left, and they were fast diminishing.

Most often I thought of her with a passion as depressing as it was consuming. I had stopped calling her; I did not want to make a nuisance of myself. But I always hoped that she would ring me up one day and tell me she wanted to come for dinner. But she never called.

Days went by. I didn't know what was happening and I was too vain to ask anybody about it. The early spring dissolved into rain as it so often does in New England. And, with the rain, cold returned once more.

With the coming of cold a strange desperation grew upon me. My love for June was streaked with hatred and anger. And with every passing day my love fed upon my anger and both grew stronger. It was as if two high voltage electrodes had taken root in my head and each of them kept spitting venom into my brain. The strain grew so great that I almost lost all ability to think logically for any length of time. Often I suspected I was going mad.

I tried to concentrate on my work. I suspended all my experiments because I just did not have the concentration to carry them out. I tried to read in the library but on the very first page I would get lost in thoughts of June and Babu and myself, and hours went by without my making any headway. I tried to compare myself with what I had been before I met June and the difference seemed so great that I laughed. I had become possessive, selfish and greedy—all that I had struggled against for years. But the realisation was of little help, considering the fact that I had almost lost my will power. I had permitted myself to become a battlefield where the child and the adult warred unceasingly. The child usually came on top.

Sometimes I tried to console myself with the fact that June would have had to leave me some day anyway. She was foolish to go for Babu, but he would at least take good care of her. But, more often, I just refused to believe that she had left me or was going to leave me. And all this time the thought of offering her marriage as a price of retaining her never struck me. That would have been too hypocritical, even in my desperate condition.

All this conflict left me immensely strained and it was in such a condition one evening that I decided to call her. I didn't want to use the lab telephone since others would have overheard me. I decided to call from the street.

It was cold outside and a slight drizzle descended from a leaden sky. I didn't have my overcoat with me and I shivered as I walked down the street. A young girl was busy with the telephone. I couldn't hear what she was saying but she was apparently flirting with somebody. Minutes passed and she kept pouring money into the telephone. I stood outside, my arms locked together in an effort to keep warm. At last she finished and got out.

"Sorry," she said, smiling as she brushed past me; she had apparently won that round.

June picked up the phone. She sounded pleasantly surprised to hear my voice.

"We thought you had gone out somewhere," she said.

We, indeed! I said I was very much in town, although I had been planning to go out. We chattered for a while. Then I said, "I want to see you, June."

There was a silence. Perhaps she was thinking.

"I was wondering if we could have dinner together tonight."

"I'm sorry, Sindi. I will not be able to see you anymore, I mean not as I used to. Babu and I are getting married soon."

There was a long pause. The pendulum had swung at last and I had been removed by its stroke.

"Can't I see you just once?"

"No, Sindi, I am sorry." She sounded genuinely pained at having to say that.

"All right," I said.

I heard the click of the telephone as she hung up. I put down the receiver. Then pressing my face against the cold, hard metal of the telephone, I cried. I cried silently and hopelessly until a knock on the glass door indicated that I was wasting somebody's time.

Part Three

Part Three

11

*F*OR MANY days after Mr. Ghosh first visited us, there was a busy stir in the office. The income tax man's visit was discussed all over the place. You found them in the toilet and the cyclostyling room and the crumbling tea shop downstairs where we had tea twice a day, discussing, discussing, discussing. I think Indians discuss things more than any other people. The tiny, shrunken accountant, who was Mr. Khemka's confidential man, suddenly found himself very popular.

Mr. Khemka was nowhere to be seen. Both he and Sheila had gone to one of those holiday resorts in the hills. I have often wondered what on earth these big people do when they get up to these God-forsaken villages. I would understand if artists and thinkers and writers were to go there, but what the hell do these businessmen do there besides talk about their health and shake their money bags?

Anyway Mr. Khemka showed up towards the end of the month, all bright and cheery with a new haircut. He was a good-looking old fox. The first thing he did was give everybody a piece of his mind. After he had given me the going-over I told him I had something to tell him. He said if I wanted to talk to him at leisure I could come and have dinner with him. I wanted to tell him about the gossip going around the office and would rather have finished with it right there, but he seemed busy, so I decided to go along to his house.

I told him what I had heard the clerks say. He said it was all nonsense. The Income Tax Department had some misunderstanding which would soon be cleared. He said his company was one of the

115

best rated by the government. The lower classes would always talk. Then he added confidentially, "Take a tip from me, Sindi. Never trust the lower classes. They have to be made use of, but kept in their place."

I said I didn't quite see what a man's class had to do with the amount of gossip he generated. What was more, it seemed to me, there was cause for some concern as to the way things were going.

Mr. Khemka smiled patronisingly and said, "You are young, Sindi, and you are new to this country. You don't really know what's what. These things go on. People always talk. A shrewd businessman takes them in his stride."

Then he got off on his advice-giving session, which was normal when he managed to scrape up enough affection for somebody. He started off by saying that I should be more discriminating and that I shouldn't mix with all and sundry. I suppressed a yawn. Sheila had apparently been delayed somewhere in the dressing rooms of that palace. She might even have lost her way. Mr. Khemka was rattling on pompously. I suppose he got irritated because he did not find me responsive, because he suddenly turned on me and said,

"The trouble with you foreign-returned chaps is that you think no end of yourselves."

Perhaps he didn't know that I certainly thought rather poorly of myself.

"Take your case for example. I can't make head or tail out of you. I grant you that you are not a stuffed shirt, but then you are stubborn as a mule. Even mules mend their ways if they are beaten enough, but nothing seems to affect you."

I had a fairly good idea what he had in mind but I suddenly wanted to provoke him further. I looked up at him, pretending to be completely lost.

"Don't look at me like that," Mr. Khemka snapped. "You jolly well know what I am talking about."

That was his favourite expression. Whenever he was angry things became "jolly well" for him.

"What is wrong with you anyway?" he asked, leaning forward in his chair and putting his hand on my knee.

"Don't you have any ambitions?"

I told him I used to have ambition but I didn't anymore.

"But why, why?" he exclaimed, throwing his hand all over the place. "Don't you want to become a director of the Company some day?"

"No," I said, and that was the fact.

I wished I hadn't come. I wondered why Sheila was taking so long. Just at that moment she entered and sat down by the door. I smiled at her and she smiled back. In her own house she was like a pet animal which went about where it willed, confident of not being noticed.

"Look here, Sindi," Mr. Khemka said. "I have spent thirty years more than you in this world. You'll agree with me that I know a lot about it. You must tell me what is bothering you. I might be able to help you."

"Nothing is bothering me, Mr. Khemka."

"Then why are you so strange?"

"I'm not strange. I am perhaps different from you and your world. My set of experiences has taught me a reality that is different from yours. That's all. And then... ." I was in a mood to continue but I didn't know how it would be received.

"And then, what?"

"And then America did strange things to me just as it did strange things to Babu."

"Babu was a fool," Mr. Khemka growled.

I poured myself another drink.

"You are too harsh on him, Papa," Sheila said. "Babu was young and innocent. Other people took advantage of him."

It was just this kind of naivete that puzzled me. It even made me a little angry. I said,

"Nobody took advantage of him. It is the innocent who take advantage of others and Babu was one of them. He didn't know what he was doing; nor did you, for that matter. It was as much your fault. You sent him to America without knowing what you were doing."

"Nonsense," Mr. Khemka said. That was another word he liked. "Nonsense. I had sent him to study. I had sent him to one of the best universities of America. It was not my fault that he got entangled with strange women and ended up in a car accident."

I looked at him passively. The whisky had pushed me into a calm stratosphere. Beneath the anger I could barely see the touch of remorse, the lingering doubt. And the doubt spread to me. Much as I would have liked to pin the blame on somebody, the doubt held me by the throat like a mad dog.

I said, "It was nobody's fault and it was everybody's fault. You

117

had given him the wrong set of memories. He wanted to get away from them but memories are vicious little things, Mr. Khemka. They make little fortifications in your soul. You can't get rid of them unless you destroy them and destroy yourself in the process."

"So that's what Babu did?" It was Sheila who spoke.

"Yes! That's what Babu did! And that is what I am doing. I still have a chance. Not a big one, I admit, yet it is a chance one can bank upon until the last minute."

A mournful silence hit the room. All of us had had our say for the time being. Mr. Khemka looked baffled. Now and again he glanced at me, trying to make sure that I was not drunk. 'I don't understand,' his whole being seemed to say. Shiela sat in her corner, waiting silently. She appeared moved. Perhaps the mention of Babu's name had done the trick. Babu's name always seemed to unlock some hidden portals in her consciousness. The big clock in the dining room ticked loudly while each of us pursued his own train of thought. Finally, Mr. Khemka spoke.

"I don't understand all this. I don't understand it at all. God only knows what is coming over you young people."

I said that so far as I could see it was not a matter of youth. It was just what you go through and how sensitive you are.

Mr. Khemka said, "Don't tell me I haven't gone through as much as any of you youngsters. When we were young we fell in love with girls next door but we didn't make an ass of ourselves."

"But you at least knew what made an ass of a man; we don't even know that. You had a clear-cut system of morality, a caste system that laid down all you had to do. You had a God; you had roots in the soil you lived upon. Look at me. I have no roots. I have no system of morality. What does it mean to me if you call me an immoral man. I have no reason to be one thing or another. You ask me why I am not ambitious; well, I have no reason to be. Come to of it I don't even have a reason to live!"

The little speech left me breathless. I was surprised at my own eloquence. The whisky was really doing the trick. For a while everyone was quiet. Then Sheila spoke.

"But Babu was different," she said. "He had ambition and he had a reason for living. He knew how much we all loved him and he had all these factories to come back to."

They all made the same mistake. They thought factories gave everybody a reason for living just because they gave Mr. Khemka a reason to live.

I said she was perhaps right. Babu was different. He had roots and he had a God. But they had sent him out before his God could take care of him. They had almost wanted him to destroy his roots. In the end he didn't have any reason to live either.

"That is not true," Mr. Khemka said. "We never wanted him to do anything of the sort. It was bad influence on him that led him astray."

I sighed. How could anyone answer that? And maybe he was right. Maybe June and I had been bad influence. How could I know?

"I had brought him up with all the care that a father can give to a child," Mr. Khemka went on. "Even as a child I had myself taught him what was right and what was wrong. How could have I, who had given him roots, wanted him to destroy them? It is ridiculous. I had wanted him to gain some polish, yes. But how would I have known he would abandon all his morality in the process?"

The touch of remorse was gone from his voice. He sounded strangely matter-of-fact, as if he were discussing a piece of equipment of someone else's son.

I said, "Your morality was nice for India. It didn't work in America. That's why I say you gave him a wrong set of memories."

"What would you have taught him?" Mr. Khemka said, retaliating suddenly.

What would have I taught him? The question puzzled me. What would I have taught him?

I said, "I don't know. Nothing perhaps. I would have asked him to go into the world and make up his own mind."

"Then he would have been like you. Living, but as good as dead."

"Father," Sheila interrupted suddenly. "Don't say that. Sindi is not dead."

I looked at her in amazement. She felt my gaze and began to blush. A feeling of tenderness rose within me. For no apparent reason I remembered the day I had held her on the staircase of Wengers. Mr. Khemka looked at her and then at me. He sighed and shrugged his shoulders.

"Oh, let us eat now. We have had enough of this pointless discussion."

After dinner Mr. Khemka left us together. When we had settled down to coffee and I had begun to enjoy the evening, Sheila asked suddenly,

"Don't you have any reason to live?"

"Oh, I like drinking coffee after dinner and I like sitting with you."

"No, seriously, haven't you any reason to live?"

I didn't want to answer the question, yet it was the kind of question that can stir you up if the mood is right and the right person asks it. Temptation for self-pity is stronger than the devil. I looked at Sheila; she seemed earnest and sincere. This was the first time she had shown any interest in me.

I said I didn't really. Not in the usual sense, anyway.

"Isn't there anything you want?"

As I sipped my coffee I wondered how to answer that one. I was like the dull school boy who always gets stuck with the same unanswerable questions.

There were things I wanted, only I didn't know how to get them. I wanted the courage to live as I wanted; the courage to live without desire and attachment. I wanted peace and perhaps a capacity to love. I wanted all these. But above all, I wanted to conquer pain. What could I have done with the directorship of a company if the ball of pain still hung around my neck like a dead albatross? I wanted an answer to the questions that my suffering had left with me like swollen carcasses on a river bank after a flood. Only after I knew what my purpose was, could I begin to fulfil it.

"There are many things I want, Sheila, I couldn't tell you all, the list is too long."

"Tell me some."

I said I would have liked to conquer pain if it was possible. "I can't stand it," I added.

"Is that why you withdraw from all action that might cause pain?"

"Perhaps. But I withdraw from action for another reason. I first want to know the purpose of action."

"But that would be purpose of life itself."

"No. It needn't be. There is no purpose in life. There is perhaps a little purpose in right action, in action without desire."

"Perhaps you want to become a saint," Sheila said smiling.

I said I had little desire to become a saint. I merely wanted to escape pain. I had tried many ways but I had found none.

Then she said what they all tell you in India sooner or later.

"Perhaps you ought to get married."

"I have tried that also," I said grinning.

"What? Have you been married?"

Sheila looked surprised.

"No." I laughed. "I haven't been married. But I've loved women. I have even lived with them. But it always ended. The holidays and the travels, tender love-making before going to sleep, it all ended in emptiness."

"Did they leave you?"

"We never left. It all fizzled out like an ill-packed cracker. I never let them love me."

"How can anyone do that?"

"A woman never loves a man who doesn't need her."

"Didn't you ever need them?"

"I perhaps did. But I pretended I didn't. I couldn't pay the price of being loved."

I paused. I must be drunk, I said to myself. I didn't know why I was talking so much. I looked at the sculptures, seeking an answer to my strange loquaciousness but they only stared back at me. For some reason I suddenly felt depressed. Inside me alcohol mingled with my blood, pushing me to the edge of loneliness. Sheila sat huddled in a corner dreaming of her brother. Mr. Khemka perhaps snored upstairs. The stone-women stared voluptuously, their hips poised for the acts of love.

Sheila was silent. But she was thinking. And what she was thinking soon became apparent.

"Haven't you ever been in love?"

It was a woman's question. Yet I wanted to answer it. The sadness was slowly growing upon me and I wanted to talk.

I said, "I have been in love, in my own way. And I will never love like that again."

"Why?"

"It's too painful."

"Did she hurt you?"

"No, not really. But I hurt myself. I suddenly found that I wanted to possess a human being. And all the while I knew I couldn't do it. Nobody can do it."

"Why should all that be painful?"

Sheila looked puzzled.

"Have you ever been in love?" I asked.

It was only when I saw her blushing that I realised one should never ask such a question of an Indian girl.

"No," she said softly.

I said, "How can I tell you then what it feels like to take somebody's love for granted and then one day realise that she doesn't want you anymore? It breaks your heart, if you know what that means."

"But one can try again, can't one?"

"I suppose one could. But things are just not the same. Life is not a business account, losses of which can be written off against the gains. Once your soul goes bankrupt, no amount of plundering can enrich it again."

There was a long pause. Then Sheila said, "You are the saddest man I have ever known. I don't know what's the matter with you but you'll forget."

She paused for a while. Then she said, "I think it is raining."

I strained to hear. Outside, the wind sighed in the trees and rain fell in an almost silent shower. Sheila said I would forget what bothered me. It was ironic indeed. Could I ever forget Babu as long as I watched her brooding over his death? The cat jumped onto the sofa and purred expectantly. The rain increased. Some more rivers would be flooded by tomorrow. A car roared through the back lane. Absent-mindedly I watched the clock. It was almost eleven. I didn't want to talk any more. I felt drained, like the coffee cups. The dregs still stuck to the bottom but no amount of alcohol could ever draw them out. Sheila came with me to the porch, and for a while we stood on the verandah watching the rain. Lightning flashed continually, revealing the dark tree shapes.

Suddenly Sheila reached out and caught hold of my arm. She said.

"Time is a great healer."

However deeply one might feel, it always boils down to a cliche, a proverb from the high school grammar. I wanted to tell her I was not particularly sad but it was nice of her to say that.

Then she said, "You are still a foreigner. You don't belong here."

That is what Mr. Ghosh had said. Ghosh! I had almost forgotten about him. Now I remembered him like the ugly smell picked up near an open manhole. I said,

"Ghosh has caused quite a stir in the office."

"Has he?" Sheila looked more worried than her father.

"Is it pretty serious?"

122

"I don't know, Sindi. I would rather not talk about it. I don't know what is going to happen."

Then she said good night and was gone.

I stood alone in the verandah, thinking of Ghosh.

When I drove out, the rain had stopped but water stood on the streets, reflecting the shabby street lights. And I had a distinct feeling that we had not yet seen the last of Mr. Ghosh.

12

AFTER JUNE left me it was lucky I had my work to go back to; otherwise the emptiness that surrounded me would have been unbearable. For a while it left me completely dazed. I suppose for other people these things come as a blow and they cry or get drunk or go to bed with a prostitute. For me it was just one long coma. It was as if somebody had given me a big dose of anaesthesia. The edge of pain, I imagine, was so intense that it left me numb. I had known all along that June would go away some day, but I didn't realise she had already become a part of me. Our separation had been like an unforeseen abortion.

For a week or so I just lay in my room doing nothing. Karl had gone away to Chicago or I would have caused him considerable embarrassment. Gradually, however, the coma wore off and I became aware of the raw wounds. I started going out and, where I had earlier remained cooped up in my apartment, I now began to spend the whole day outside. I consciously kept clear of the places where June and I used to go together but occasionally I would run into an old landmark, a cafe or a theatre or a stretch of the beach, and I would say to myself: Here is where we met, here I bought her a book, there she wanted me to kiss her, and my heart would sink with the burden of my memories and I couldn't help whispering to myself, "My darling! Oh, my darling!"

But I soon grew accustomed to the wounds. In a way I was an old hand at this and, even as the wounds bled, some of my old will power returned. There is nothing that replenishes my will more than the realisation that the past cannot be redeemed. And this realisation had at last come home to me. It was surprising that it should have taken so long. But it was at last there, and like a castrated bull I returned to the yoke of everyday life, for whatever it was worth.

I went to the labs before sunrise and stayed until sheer physical exhaustion forced me to go home. Sometimes I didn't even have strength to get up and go home. On such occasions I stretched my legs on a stool and went to sleep in the lab itself. My professor was surprised at this sudden turn in my scholastic efficiency. He didn't say it, but whenever I met him I could see the faint twinkle of speculation behind the thick lenses. One day he came to the lab and sat down beside me.

"What has come over you, Sindi? You have suddenly turned a scholar," he said. I couldn't help laughing. "I have just discovered that I am a genius, Professor, and I want to make the best of it."

"You are not trying to get away from something, are you?"

"We all are, aren't we? Once you are born, you spend the rest of your life getting away from your birth."

He was quiet for a while. I don't think he had heard me.

Then he said, "Life is very long and you are still young."

"Too long, sir, much too long, with payments that are much too heavy for weak men."

"You can always pay in instalments," he said dreamily, puffing at his pipe.

"You can. But some of us don't want to be debtors."

"You are quite a philosopher, aren't you?"

"No." I said. "I am just trying to forget something."

"I thought so," he said and got up to leave.

"Have you thought about the offer I made you about joining the faculty here?"

"Yes, I have," I said, "I think I'd rather go to New York."

"We'll miss you, you know."

I thought I too would miss Boston, but for different reasons. He paused near the door and turned towards me.

"Why don't you come and stay with us for a while? My wife will be glad to have you."

I looked up at him a trifle surprised. This Nobel Prize winner who lived in the world of mathematics and electrons was more humane than the beatniks and philosophers who spent their lives gibbering about pain.

"You are very kind, sir, but I would rather be alone. Thanks a lot anyway."

"Take care of yourself," he said.

I said I would, but he was already gone, fumbling shortsightedly through the landing.

For a whole month I continued to work and I even achieved a few major breakthroughs in my project. With the coming of spring my asthma returned and what with the kind of life I was leading, my health went rapidly to pieces. It hurt me physically and people advised me to take rest; but they didn't know that it was the hurt of memories and not physical pain that I dreaded. And, whenever I paused to rest, memories came roaring back in a maddening procession.

It was during this time that I met Babu in the student cafeteria. Had I seen him earlier, I would have moved away, but I spotted him only when he came and sat down right next to me.

"Hi, Sindi. Haven't seen you for a long time." He had begun to put on the American accent. "How are you?" I wondered if I heard a note of triumph in his voice but it was probably my imagination.

"I am all right."

"You look pulled down." Little balls of jam formed at the corners of his mouth as he munched his doughnuts.

"Do I?" I said trying to laugh.

"Yes. Is something the matter?"

Did he really not know? Or, was he just being sarcastic? Hadn't June told him about ourselves? Babu could put on an act, but it was not very likely.

"June and I are getting married, you know," he said with a touch of pride.

"I know. June told me about it. Congratulations."

"Do you think I have made the right choice?" His innocence was driving me to exasperation.

"She has nice breasts," I said.

Babu looked up at me with hurt dog-like eyes and I suddenly felt ashamed of myself.

"I am sorry, Babu," I said. "I didn't mean it. I am glad you are marrying her. I am sure she'll make you happy. She is a wonderful girl."

Babu brightened up at once. It was strange that even now he should look up to me for approval. Didn't he know that he was the victor?

"I am throwing a party for our engagement. Would you like to come?"

"I'll try to come. When is it?"

125

He gave me the time and place. It was one of those expensive hotels where Republicans meet to gather money.

"You must come," Babu said again grasping my hand. "Promise me that you'll come." To cut the matter short, I promised I'd come.

I went, not because I had promised Babu, but because I wanted to see June again. She stood in the doorway, beautiful with her hair brushed back like a school girl. To my surprise she had put on a sari to mark the Indianness of the occasion. I wanted to tell her that she looked beautiful, but I thought it might be misunderstood.

"How thin you have grown!" she exclaimed, grasping my hand in both of her own. I wondered if she remembered saying that to me once before.

"Have I?" I said, pretending surprise.

"Yes, sir, you have. What have you been doing with yourself?"

"Nothing much."

"You have been working too hard."

There was nothing to say in reply to that. Another couple waited behind me to greet June and I moved on.

It was the same old International Students Association crowd—Indians, Pakistanis, Koreans. Americans who wanted to know more about India, Japanese who wanted to know more about Americans, a few girls from June's office, Babu's professor, Mrs. Blyth, a heavily painted old woman whom nobody seemed to know and who later turned out to be Babu's landlady. Neither of us seemed to belong there; that was may be why I started talking to her.

"Isn't he wonderful?" she said in a loud, squeaky voice.

"Who is?"

"I was talking of Babu."

"Is he?" She looked dumbfounded.

"Well, isn't he?"

"I suppose he is," I said grinning.

We talked at random like two blind persons feeling for each other's face. She said Indians were an exotic people with wonderful eyes. She had been a landlady for thirty years and she had never had a tenant as polished and polite as Babu. She asked where I was from. I told her.

"You are not Sindi?" she exclaimed, looking me up and down as if it was quite impossible for anyone like me to have that name.

"I am," I said.

"But Babu simply adores you!" she squeaked loudly, her pale grey eyes bursting with disbelief.

126

"The only snag is he adores my girl, too."

"You shouldn't say such things in public," the old lady said lowering her voice to a discreet whisper. She looked around the room and went on, "What would his fiancee think if she heard you?" To cut her short, I said I was sorry and walked away.

A group of Indian students stood in a corner fumbling with their coffee cups. They all had their eyes on June, and I could see the shadow of envy and sadness in their eyes. They were talking about Babu and June.

"Babu is a bloody fool. He should have just played with her instead of getting hooked like that," one of them said. He was a tall Sikh who had shaved. And he used to say that the Sikhs were the most virile of all Indian people.

"What did she see in him anyway? She is so pretty, she could have married almost anybody."

They chattered like a bunch of post-graduate monkeys, commenting on what was wrong with Babu and June and what they should have done instead of getting married. Periodically, one of them cut a crude joke and they shook hands with each other. I watched them, because I had nothing else to do. Suddenly the shaved Sikh turned to me.

"Say didn't you use to go out with her?"

"Yes, we have been friends."

"Intimate friends?"

"I don't know what you mean by intimate friends."

"Did you sleep with her?" he said grinning broadly at me.

"No," I said.

They all looked relieved and went back to their gossip. I listened to them for a while and then I walked away. I felt tired and strained. There was absolutely nobody I could talk to. At the same time I didn't want to go away. I wanted to be near June as long as possible. It was like an opium-eater's addiction, and I knew that like an opium-eater I couldn't help it. I got another cup of coffee and sat down in a corner. June hopped girlishly from person to person talking vivaciously, introducing Babu to friends, meeting Babu's friends, showing off her sari to a crowd of admirers. I wondered where she had got hold of it. It looked very expensive with all the gold. I watched her with amusement, forgetting for a moment my own loneliness. The spell was broken by a stumbling whisper.

"Aren't they adorable?"

It was the little Japanese biochemist. The way she pronounced "adorable" I suspected she had just picked it up.

"Hullo," I said.

"I am happy to see you again."

I didn't know what she meant, so I just smiled.

"You have a beautiful smile. A little cheerful, a little sad, and very sexy."

"Aren't they adorable!" I said to change the topic.

"What did I tell you four months ago? Didn't I tell you they were very much in love," she said.

I nodded. She seemed to take as much pride in it as if a great breakthrough in biochemistry, prophesied by her, had come true.

"I like international marriages. That is the only way to have one world."

"Is that really necessary?" I said.

"Without that, life is nonsense."

"There are other things that make nonsense of life."

"You talk bitter."

"Nothing serious." I said. "Just a passing thought."

We chatted irrelevantly for a while. Then she said she had to go.

The crowd had thinned considerably. A broad-hipped maid in a blue frock went around the room gathering empty coffee cups. I got up and prepared to leave.

"Don't go away so early," June said when I went to say good-bye.

"I am almost the last one," I said looking around.

"Wait a while," she said putting her hand on my arm. "Let everybody go. Then we'll go over to the house and have some fun, just three of us."

Like an opium-addict I waited for my pill. After everybody was gone we got into a huge, white convertible and drove off.

"Whose car is this?" I asked.

"I bought it yesterday," Babu said proudly.

"Isn't she beautiful?" June said.

I nodded. With the new monstrosity thrown in, the balance of love must be completely tilted.

"I love cars," June said gaily.

That was almost all she loved, I wanted to say; but I knew that wouldn't be true and I didn't have the courage to hurt myself.

Babu was full of plans for the future. He seemed to be in high spirits, and in a way I was glad to be with him. While we sat around

Mrs. Blyth's living room he related to me all that he had in mind for June and himself. He said he would get married in August as soon as his summer school was over, and then they would both go out on a long tour of the U.S.A. with a special holiday in New Orleans where June had always wanted to go. He told me he had already written to the American Automobile Association for details regarding his tour plan. He had also written to some of his friends in California, and they all seemed very excited about his marriage as well his forthcoming visit to California.

June was silent all this while. I had a feeling that some of her gaiety was gone and she was feeling slightly strained. Her gaze kept flitting from one to the other of us without registering.

Judging from the way Babu had behaved towards me so far I came to the conclusion that June had not told him about ourselves. This, I thought, was best under the circumstances. It would have hurt Babu unnecessarily to know about it, especially since the whole thing had ended.

When Babu had finished I asked him casually whether he had any plans to visit his family in India. He said he had none at the moment but the question seemed to put him off. It must have been about this time that he wrote the second letter to Sheila. Even June looked more strained than before. I had a feeling they were angry with me for asking the question. I felt rather awkward at this since I had not meant it that way.

After this I wasn't sure what to say to them. The question uppermost on my mind concerned my own loneliness, but I didn't want to discuss that. I could have been mistaken, but I had a feeling that June would have liked to say a few things if Babu had not been there. However, since he *was* there, we spent another half hour in small talk and then I said that I had to go. They wanted me to stay for dinner, but I had to go to the labs since I had left my experiment running.

One evening some days later while I sat reading at my flat, the door bell rang and Babu walked in. He looked unkempt and crestfallen. I made him a drink and he sat down near the window. He started talking about his studies. He seemed nervous and vacant, as one tends to look after pointlessly worrying about a situation that cannot be remedied. He had received a severe warning from one of his professors. Babu had been told that he might have to leave the college if he didn't improve.

"Are you really trying to improve?" I asked.

Babu said he had been working very hard but nothing seemed to make any difference. He said he had been a good student in India, but in America the method of working was so different that he didn't know how to cope with it.

"Hasn't your engagement to June made any difference?" I asked.

"It has. I feel a totally different man. It is wonderful to get married. You ought to get married."

The fool, that was not what I had wanted to hear.

"Hasn't it made any difference to your studies?"

He said it had, but the way he said it, I had a feeling he was lying. Anyway, I didn't want to pursue it since it was none of my business.

Babu seemed to slide back into deep thought and I went back to my reading.

After a while he spoke again.

"I am really worried about my father, Sindi," he said adopting a mocking gay style but his face betrayed the fear.

Since I had nothing to say I kept quiet.

"If they throw me out of school this time, my father might never want to see me again."

"Well, don't see him," I said. "Are you afraid of losing the inheritance?"

Babu looked horrified as if I had uttered an unbelievable blasphemy.

"Are you crazy?" he said pronouncing the word with perfect American intonation.

"Not any more than you or your father."

"Don't talk of my father like that," Babu said, breaking into Hindi. He always spoke Hindi when he was angry.

He went on to say that I was a conceited little squirt who didn't know what a Hindu family was like. What is worse, he said, I was a perfect example of an Indian who pretended to be a foreigner and behaved as one.

I asked him what he expected me to do.

"I had come here just to talk things over with you because I thought you were my friend. But I'll go if you don't want me to stay."

"Don't be a fool, Babu," I said in exasperation. "Why don't you grow up for a change? Why do you have to come in here every few weeks and cry like a child over your studies? If you don't have the

130

guts to do anything about it you might as well face the facts. You are not in fairyland where you can get what you want just by wishing it. It is high time you ceased to be an innocent little rich-father's-boy and got down to doing something."

I had had enough of the whole lot of them and he was going to hear what I thought of his father.

"And that father of yours... ."

"Don't speak of my father!" Babu interrupted.

"I don't care a damn of what happens to you or to him. But let me tell you this: unless you grow up and get him out of your system, this country is going to grind your face right into its grubby trash cans and no one will even notice." There was a long silence in which Babu stared at his toes. I trembled to think of what June would do if she suddenly discovered one day that she had married a kid.

"You are getting married soon, Babu," I said in a quieter tone. "You are involving one more person. And your innocence can now devastate both of you."

"I have not come here for a sermon, Sindi. I know I am getting married, and I don't think I need any advice from you, of all people."

Somehow it hurt, and I had a feeling that Babu knew that it did. I, of all people, was not fit to give advice. I said nothing. I had hurt him and could I blame him if he sought to wound me in turn? Looking at him sitting there in his elegant suit, I was suddenly struck by the difference between us. I was cynical and exhausted, grown old before my time, weary with my own loneliness. Babu was young and looked forward to a life of pleasure in which men like me only travelled now and then as advisers. They had no right to any emotions and, if they showed any, they even lost their meagre status as advisers.

"Go home," I said in anger. "Go home and hide your face in your pillow. Don't come to me for advice. I am not interested in your sob stories. I never was and never will be. You mean nothing to me. And that father of yours who has made this bloody mess of you, tell him to come and wipe your tears for you. I have had enough of you. You...,"

Suddenly Babu got up and flung his glass into the fireplace. His chest heaved as he tried to keep himself from crying. The shattering glass broke the spell of anger. I realised how petty I was. But Babu had already left and I could hear his hurried, uneven steps on the stairs as he went down. I wanted to go after him and call him back, but my pride prevented me. I went over to the window and watched him go

131

down the road. He paused once to blow his nose and perhaps to wipe a tear. That was the last time I saw him alive.

A few weeks later I was called for my oral examinations. It was rather amusing the way we spent four hours discussing things which hardly mattered to the universe and about which I personally did not care a damn.

After the examination was over they all congratulated me and shook my hand. One of them even called me Doctor Oberoi. Before parting they asked me whether I had enjoyed my stay at the college. I said I didn't know but it appeared to be as good a way of spending a chunk of one's life as any other.

"I'm sure you would be of immense help to your country. They badly need people like you."

I would have liked to know which country he was referring to.

Before leaving, the chairman asked me if there was anything else I wished I had learnt at the college.

"I wish I had been taught how to live, Professor," I said tiredly.

At this they all laughed as if it was the funniest thing in the world.

I went home and started packing.

It was like an auctioneer's retirement; much had been auctioned and whatever remained was of little value. Yet it had to be carried along like a heap of rotting memories. I took out the battered suitcases that I had brought along from London a few years before. I rummaged through the house picking up little odds and ends and stacking them in neat little rows. Each little inanimate thing breathed with memories that were as much a part of me as the regular thudding of my heart. A cardboard box worn on the edges fell on the floor disgorging a bunch of old photographs. A picture of my parents just after their wedding; the headmaster's wife in Nairobi who had wanted to be a mother to me; a photograph of Kathy near one of the lakes in Scotland; skiing in Switzerland with Judy and Christine. They didn't know I had carried on with both of them. How clever I had thought I was, but, in the end both of them had hated me. The Chinese girl in San Francisco. There was a time when I used to count them like soldiers counted heads in the old days. And then one day I had got up and found how gory it all was.

Going through another drawer I found an old bracelet that I had bought for June. She had taken it off one night because it hurt my back when I made love to her. I looked at it with a mixture of sadness and tenderness. It was like a monument commemorating a burial and yet it drew me. I wondered what to do with it. At first I thought I'd return it to her, but then I decided to keep it.

It was almost midnight when I finished packing. I went around the empty rooms once again and then sat down to have a beer. Doctor Oberoi, indeed. It sounded strange. I wondered if all doctors were like me: little children who had started going to school at five and didn't know how to stop. And when one considered that some of these doctors were even responsible for running the world, one was not surprised at the mess we were in.

Suddenly the telephone rang. It was June. Her voice came unclear because of the loud baying of a juke box in the background.

"Babu and I are going to the beach tomorrow. Would you like to come? It would be lots of fun."

"Have you asked Babu?" I said.

"No. But I am sure he won't mind. You will come, won't you."

"I would have liked to come, June, but I am leaving for New York tomorrow."

"For how long?"

"For good, I am afraid."

There was a pause in which only the juke box played and I heard her blow her nose. I had a sudden suspicion that she had been drinking. June drank rarely and then only when she was badly depressed.

"I...We'll miss you," she said.

"Where are you speaking from, June?"

"From a bar in the Square, I came here with some girls from the office."

There was another long pause. Neither of us had the courage to put the receiver down. Then she spoke again.

"Will you be coming to Boston on visits?"

I said, "As a matter of fact I will. The project I am to take up in New York is connected with some people here."

"Do look us up when you come."

I said I would.

"God bless you," she said.

"Take care of yourself, my love," I whispered, but she had already hung up.

I had no particular interest in the work I was assigned to do in New York, but I discovered that my colleagues depended upon me. Moreover, there were certain things that only I could do. Under these circumstances, not to have done my bit would have been letting them down unnecessarily. So I got interested, and a stage came when I was only aware of my work and of nothing else, not even of June or Babu.

The only time I was fully aware of their existence was when I visited Boston every few weeks. I never looked them up as I had promised because I had nothing to say to them and it would have been awkward for everybody. Some of my old tranquillity returned. Again I had come face to face with the lusty beast in me and slowly came to forgive him.

The date for Babu's wedding came and went. I had bought a little present for them but there was no point in sending it when I didn't get an invitation.

One day when I was in Boston I ran into June in the old cafe near the university. She had her back to me and I decided to go to a different restaurant, but she turned and saw me standing in the doorway. Reluctantly, I walked towards her.

She got up and took my hand in both of hers.

"Oh, Sindi, how nice to see you."

"Nice to see *you*, June," I said.

"Oh, come on, you liar."

"When did you come?" she asked.

"Two days ago."

"Is this the first time?"

I hesitated. "No, I came here before."

There was a long silence as if we had suddenly exhausted all that we had to say.

"How did the wedding go?" I said.

"Oh, the wedding. We have postponed it for a while." Her voice sounded hollow.

I wanted to ask her if something had gone wrong, but it was none of my business. We talked about her work and her mother and many other topics that men rely upon to fill in the silences of their lives. From all appearances I assumed that the June I was talking to was the same that I had known earlier. But soon I became aware that something had changed. I couldn't identify it, and it disturbed me. The

134

expression in her eyes frequently went blank and she lost the thread of her conversation. Her laugh was forced, and I noticed that she was heavily made up.

"Are you worried about something, June?" I said.

"We all have our little problems, Sindi, like you used to say."

I laughed and she laughed with me, but it was the laugh of a person who had come to realise the sadness of living.

"How is Babu?" I asked in order to change the topic.

"He is all right. Working hard for his exams. I must go and see him now."

I wanted to ask her if he was still angry with me, but it was a pointless question which had only one answer.

"Try and see us next time you are in Boston," she said, getting up.

I nodded.

A few hours later I left for New York and didn't return for some weeks. At times I thought of June for hours together, speculating on what could be bothering her. But there was no way of knowing, and ultimately I wrote off the matter as something I could do nothing about.

When I went to Boston again, an irrepressible desire to see June seized me. I couldn't bring myself to go back to New York without finding out whether she was really unhappy. In some naive way I believed that I might be able to help her solve her problems. Innocence, as I can see now, was not only Babu's bane.

I called her at the office. She said Babu wasn't free until late in the evening and we couldn't meet until dinner. I said I was leaving by the evening flight and wanted to see her. After a moment's thought she agreed.

I picked her up at the office and we went to the restaurant where she was to meet me again a few weeks later to hear of Babu's death.

She wore a shabby blue dress and her skin had acquired an unhealthy pallor from too much worrying. We spent nearly half an hour in small talk. Then I noticed that I was running out of time. There was no point in wasting time on meaningless chit-chat, so I asked her bluntly if she was unhappy. She looked at me absent-mindedly, then said,

"I am. But how does it matter to you? Anyway, there is nothing you can do about it."

I said that I had loved her howsoever selfishly, and it hurt me to see her unhappy. She looked as if I had disclosed something that was quite unbelievable.

"What has happened to all your detachment? I thought you never loved anybody—except perhaps yourself."

"Why are you bitter, June?"

"Why should I be bitter," she said, playing with the curls on her temple.

"Don't you believe that I loved you?" I said.

"I did at one time, and perhaps still do. But you are so tied up with your detachment it makes little difference whether you love or you don't. There is nothing to be bitter about in this, it just made me sad because I thought I was in love with you."

"Are you in love with Babu now?"

"No."

"Then why did you decide to marry him?"

"I thought he needed me. I had wanted to belong to you, but you didn't want it. You are so self-sufficient there is hardly any place for me in your life—except perhaps as a mistress." She added with a short laugh.

"Babu, on the other hand, was on the edge of a breakdown—and still is for that matter. He needs me and what's more he says so. He loves me more than he loves himself—that's more than what can be said for you. In return, I am prepared to give him all that I have."

"Then what are you unhappy about."

She was quiet for a while. Then she said,

"All that I have to offer may just not be enough, Sindi."

"What does he want from you?"

"I wish to God I knew. I just don't know. Initially, I thought he just wanted me physically. When he didn't make any advances I told him he could have me whenever he felt like it. He said he didn't want to do it until after the wedding. Later on I thought that he wanted me for company, just to be there to be talked to. But now the whole thing seems to be confused. I just sit there with him every hour of the day that I can spare, aware of the immense burden of his love. I have given him all that I have, but it does not suffice. It would have been so much easier if he had just wanted my body. In five minutes it is over. A woman can see the look of satisfaction and gratitude and even feel gratified in return. But here it is just one long drawn-out agony. Each minute is loaded with the throbbing of a climax which never comes."

136

She put her elbows on the table and took her head in her hands. She reminded me of a depressing painting that I had seen in London. I had a feeling that June was crying, but the expression in her eyes when she looked up was only blank.

I leaned forward and put my hands on her arms. "Come away with me, June. Please come away with me."

"No," she said.

"You don't know what is happening to you. Babu will drive you mad."

"I must stand by him. He needs me."

"He needs much more than you can give. He'll suck your blood and marrow and leave you dead."

"It can't be any more hopeless than loving you, Sindi, can it?"

She smiled at me, slowly and steadily, her eyes that used to be so gay projecting the sadness of a martyr. As I watched her, a fierce passion rose within me, tearing me to pieces. In my agony I bent forward to kiss her as I might have kissed a child in pain. But she moved away.

"No, Sindi. Please."

The restaurant clock struck the quarter hour. I had only a few minutes to catch the plane. We parted on the pavement. I watched her thread her way through the evening crowd and disappear down a subway station.

13

ONE NIGHT, three weeks later, as I returned from the office I found a letter from June waiting for me on the doorstep. All these days she had been constantly on my mind and I grasped her letter with the ambivalent eagerness of a desperate man who is suddenly offered a gun to kill himself.

"Dear Sindi," it began, "I would much rather not have written this letter but I am fast approaching the breaking point and I suppose you are the only one I can talk to. Babu and I were not particularly cut out for each other even before, but now a strange thing has happened to him. He is just not the naive lovable little boy anymore. He has become, I wish to God I knew why, jealous and petty and irritable." (It must have been about this time that Babu wrote the last letter to Sheila.) "Whenever I see him he asks me strange questions as if he suspected me of going to bed with anybody who asked me. When he gets particularly peeved, he tells me how rich his father is and that I should consider myself fortunate to be marrying into his house. All this makes absolutely no sense to me."

"And now the last blow has fallen. Yesterday they asked him to leave the university as he has once again failed his exams. This has really broken his back. He just sits in his apartment drinking and crying. He keeps repeating that his father is going to be so ashamed of him. Sitting here in the room next to him I can hear him sobbing in his bed. I stayed here last night in fear that he might do something drastic. But he says he doesn't want me or my pity. It is really a pathetic sight, Sindi."

The remaining letter was in pencil.

"Sindi, I am utterly at a loss what to do. In such matters I used to do what you told me but you are not here and I suppose you are not interested. Anyway, it is good to have at least got it out of my system."

There were a few words about Mrs. Blyth and other common friends and then the letter ended. As I folded it back I noticed a P.S. It said, "Things look much better now that it is morning. Don't worry too much, I think I can manage things pretty well."

I was not surprised at her letter; in a way I had expected it. My first reaction after reading it was to call her on the telephone. I booked a call, but she was not at home. She was probably again sleeping at Babu's place.

I lay in bed and wondered what I was supposed to do. I would have liked to talk to June. I would have gone to Boston and tried to console her, but what purpose would it have served?

Somewhere on the floor above a clock struck midnight and presently I went to sleep fully dressed.

I slept deeply for a few hours and then awoke as suddenly as I had slept. It was not very bright but traffic had started moving in the streets. I was surprised to see myself dressed. Then events of the previous night came back to me and I once again started wondering what June expected me to do; only this time it came with a much greater force that comes only before the end of something.

138

I knew that there was very little I could do. In many ways, all that had happened was the logical termination of all that had gone before. My falling in love with June because she was what I was not; her leaving me for Babu for a dream; because I had lost the capacity to dream; and now, finally, the end of her dream. And what could I, who had so little control over his own destiny and actions, do to stem the tide whose course was set long ago?

I pondered this as I went about my morning chores, getting ready for the office. And then, while shaving I found myself thinking of the last night that June and I had spent together.

In my mind's eye I saw her naked body flushed first with desire and later trembling with remorse. The experience had passed, but the memory of my love still remained. Faintly it stirred within me. Then I decided to take the morning plane to Boston. While I could hardly stem the ebb that had already set in, I saw no harm in at least perfunctorily consoling June in her distress.

I called June from my hotel room. She was surprised. She said, "I hope you have not come because of my silly letter, Sindi."

So that was a silly letter. She certainly had a tremendous capacity for fooling herself.

"No," I lied, "I had come on business and I thought I might look you—and Babu—up." We arranged to meet in my room after she was free from the office.

We met that evening shyly, yet affectionately. I felt tongue-tied and so did she. For me she was another man's wife. I felt an unusual urge to say nothing that would displease her.

June looked prettier and healthier. But shadows of suffering still prevailed behind the big, beautiful eyes.

I asked her if she would like coffee. She said she would, and then we both fell silent. After a while I said, "Your letter disturbed me a little, June. I hope nothing is seriously wrong."

She said she had written it in a fit of self-pity and nothing was really wrong. But her eyes belied her words.

"How is your work?" she asked.

"Fine. We have just developed a machine that will throw twenty thousand people out of work and make them feel so small they will go home drunk. What more one can ask for?"

"That's cruel, isn't it?"

I said I didn't know.

"But I suppose you look at it with complete detachment." She was making fun of me.

"I hear a note of mockery in that," I said, and we both laughed. Now that I had lost her I had no images to preserve. Like an idiot without a keeper, I could afford to laugh at myself. I said,

"It is good to laugh with you again. Did I tell you, you have the most lovable laugh in town?"

"No, you didn't," she said brushing back her hair.

She appeared tired with little dark patches under her eyes that made her look like a cabaret artist.

"How is Babu?" I said.

"Not too well. But he'll be all right. We spent all day yesterday typing admission forms for about two dozen universities."

"Do you think he will succeed in getting admission?"

"We hope for the best. You should have seen the crazy reasons we gave for his getting flunked out. One of those mid-western outfits should fall for that stuff. What do you think?"

I said I didn't know. She laughed and said, "Tell me about something you do know."

"Like what?"

"Like your life in New York."

"I just told you I have got this nice little machine working."

"What do you do in the evenings?" she asked.

"Nothing," I said. "I come home, work and eat. And then I go to bed."

"Alone?"

What was the matter with her?

"Yes, alone," I said.

We bantered for another half hour. Now and then June went to the window and looked at the reddening horizon as if she expected the sky to fall down any minute. Then she suddenly said,

"Let's go for a drive, Sindi. It would be beautiful on the coast."

I agreed; I had nothing else to do.

We drove north along the New England coast. She had come in Babu's car and for some reason she wanted me to drive. It was almost like old times except that June sat away from me and we had nothing to say. She sat quietly staring out at the sunset as we raced through avenues of rich green trees. Occasionally, we passed small towns where teenage girls in over-blown frocks ate ice-cream sundaes by the roadside. As I drove I lost all awareness of June or of time. Babu's car pulsated like a restless giant under my feet and I mechanically manoeuvred it on the asphalt.

At last, when the sunset was gone and darkness had begun to gather, June said, "Shouldn't we be going back, Sindi?"

"Yes," I said. We should be going back. What else was there to do? Then I thought of something.

"Where are you having dinner?" I asked her.

"With mother."

"Why don't you have dinner with me? We could go to a small place a few miles up the road. They have pretty good food normally." June thought for a while. Then she said she didn't mind.

The place was called "The Little Hut". It was one of those high-class places where business executives brought their dates or mistresses for an evening of amorous dalliance. I knew I could ill afford it, and I took a discreet glance at my purse before going in.

They gave us a quiet corner which I supposed they gave to any couple that appeared to be in love. The headwaiter himself took our order. I wasn't hungry, but I wanted a manhattan. I was preparing to order something soft for June when she said she wanted a drink, too.

While we sipped our manhattans I started to talk about Babu again.

"Oh, Sindi, let's forget about him for a while," June pleaded. "Couldn't we talk of something else for a change. Why don't we talk about you?"

"About me? What do you want to know about me?"

"Tell me about your life in London."

"What would you like to know?"

"Anything and everything. How did you happen to go there in the first place?"

Some months before I wouldn't have answered this question, not truthfully anyway—but now I had nothing to hide. It was strange that we had never discussed it before.

"Chance," I said. "I had finished high school but I was very different from other high school boys. I had what passes for maturity. My uncle didn't know what to do with me. He thought I should go to a college in Nairobi and I even gave it a try. But it didn't quite work out. I didn't fit in. Then one evening after dinner, while we went for a walk, I told my uncle that I was contemplating suicide since I was tired of living. At first he laughed, but when he discovered that I was perfectly serious he got disturbed. He was a very understanding person and we discussed it off and on for a long time. Finally, I convinced him that my life in Nairobi had virtually ended and I might as well try my luck elsewhere. Two months later I left for London. I had no plans in mind except that, like everybody else, I was to study engineering."

I was silent for a while. I had suddenly discovered that I wanted to talk about the past. It gave me a strange sense of freedom. June was listening intently but I had almost forgotten she was there. Through the tall windows I could see where the sea touched land's edge. Staring at the unending streak of foam, I continued:

"I joined London University, but very soon I got tired of the classroom lectures. I didn't have any trouble with my courses and I passed the exams creditably enough when they came, but the question that bothered me was very different. I wanted to know the meaning of my life. And all my classrooms didn't tell me a thing about it. Ultimately, I decided that I needed experience other than studying, and I got an evening job as a dishwasher in a night club in Soho."

"Didn't you have your father's money?" June asked.

"I did. I didn't work to earn money. My mind was full of thoughts and I wanted a different kind of experience to sort my ideas out. It used to be very hot in the kitchen, especially on the dishwashing machine, but I found that amidst the clatter of pots and pans and clouds of steam I could think. I worked there for three months, until one day the manageress came along and decided that I was too delicate and polished to be a dishwasher and transferred me to the bar. It was there that one night I met Anna."

I paused. I didn't know whether to go on or not. Then June said, "Who was Anna?"

Who was Anna? It was surprising how vividly she still held my mind. People hardly know what they are talking about when they say that man forgets his painful experiences.

"Anna was a woman," I said. That was the simplest way I could describe her. "She was about thirty-five with dark hair and finely chiselled features. She was plump but pretty and looked younger than her age. She sat on the bar with a friend, but everytime I turned to look at her I found her staring at me. Just before leaving she asked me what my name was and where I was from. She came a number of times after that, and then one day she invited me to her studio."

I finished my drink and waited for another. I still remembered the long bus ride to Anna's studio as if it were yesterday. "She was a minor artist who had separated from her husband. She wanted to do a portrait of me and I felt flattered. I used to sit for her twice a week. She wanted to pay me for it but I refused. After the sitting we usually chatted over a cup of tea in her studio. She was very well read and I enjoyed talking to her. Frequently we strayed into discussing the meaning of life and what happened after death. I was shy at first, but then I told her what little I had thought about. To my surprise she listened to me with great attention and I discovered that she even admired me. Things seemed to be going all right when one day while painting she suddenly let her palette drop and she put her arms around me and started kissing me, first hesitantly and then, as I began to respond, she became feverish." June started giggling. She said,

"I can imagine you sitting there, a beautiful young morsel of twenty being seduced by a woman twice your age."

I was quiet for a while. I had a feeling June had got it all wrong, although I could not quite explain why. It wasn't at all the way she had imagined. In my mind's eye I could see Anna bending over me, her soft hands holding me behind the neck and her hot lips moving hungrily over my neck and my face and I have the distinct impression even now, as I had it then, that Anna was not yearning for me or anybody, but for her lost youth. But the sad thing about it all was that we both knew that she was never going to find it. I couldn't explain all this to June, though.

"Anyway, what did you do?"

"I was completely taken aback and I didn't know what to do. She said she loved me and that she had fallen in love with me ever since she saw me. I said I liked her very much. She wanted me to make love to her, and I did what was expected of me. But the whole thing disturbed me considerably. We carried on like this for six months. I think she loved me intensely and unselfishly. I enjoyed making love to her and her sadness attracted me, but engrossed as I was with my own self I couldn't return her love. She knew it and she thought it was her age that discouraged me. She couldn't have been farther from the truth. The thing I liked most about her was her age. Every time we made love she made me promise that I would never leave her. But we both knew it was a meaningless promise. And, ironically, it was at one of her own parties that I met Kathy."

The distinguished clientele had begun to arrive and the bustle of liveried waiters was quite a thing to see. It was strange to see middle aged man behave as I had done when I was twenty. Did man never learn or did he choose to forget what he couldn't overcome?

"Do you want to hear more?" I said smiling. June almost whispered the answer.

"Yes. Tell me about Kathy."

"She was like you, very much like you, though, perhaps a bit more realistic. Anna had fed my vanity and given me a taste for conquest. Foolish and petty that I was, I left her the moment Kathy showed any interest in me. Many months later I ran into her dead drunk in a bar with a beast of a man. I wanted to help her but it was too late. She didn't want my help. The incident left a great impression on my mind and I began to wonder about many things that I had hitherto taken for granted. A few weeks later Kathy and I parted for good; she had to go back to her husband. We imagined we were in love with each other, but she thought marriage was sacred and had to be maintained at all costs. It was all very painful and I felt miserable for days. But at the same time it marked a new beginning in my thinking."

I paused and lit a cigarette. It was strange that my memories of London should consist only of these two women. There were other women and there was the routine passing of exams and travelling in the tube trains and listening to speakers in Hyde Park. But all that never struck me as living, and the moment they were over I had forgotten them. The essence of my life in London lay in what I had learnt from Anna and Kathy. The rest had merely been supplementaries to fill in the empty hours of the day.

We had come to have our dinner, but so far we had only been drinking. June had matched me drink for drink and I had a faint suspicion she was getting high.

"Aren't you going to continue?" June asked.

"It gets rather complicated from thereon. There were a number of strands running through my life. That was the first time I came face to face with pain. Until then I had heard and read about it, but now it was real, and it seemed to permeate everything, like the smell of death in an epidemic. All that I had thought was pleasurable had ended in pain, and after all this I was as far from finding the purpose of my life as I had been to start with. It all puzzled me. And I spent a whole year wandering through the maze of my existence looking for an answer. It was not until the next summer that the answer came, not wholly but in a good enough measure, good enough to start with.

"That summer I worked in a library in a small village in Scotland and I had plenty of time to think and to read. I also made friends with

144

a Catholic priest who lived there. Initially, he had wanted to convert me—as they try to convert every Indian—but when he found that the questions bothering me were much bigger than that, he sincerely began to help me in my exploration. There never used to be much work in the library and I read a lot. In the evenings I had long talks with the priest and very often we would stay up late into the night discussing religion and God and mysticism. I have never done so much reading and thinking as I did in those three months. And then suddenly it all began to clear up."

I paused. I knew it would appear very simple to June as it now looked simple to me. But at the time it was such a revelation I had almost felt as if I had been infused with a new existence. June was waiting for me to continue, and I started once again.

"One morning I had gone for a walk. I climbed a hill and sat down on a weathered stone. The sun had just risen and the valley seemed ethereal in the clear light. Suddenly, I felt a great lightening, as if someone had lifted a burden from my chest and it all came through in a flash. All love—whether of things, or persons, or oneself— was illusion and all pain sprang from this illusion. Love begot greed and attachment, and it led to possession."

"That is not right," June said. "According to you hatred would be much better than love."

"Absence of love does not mean hatred. Hatred is just another form of love. There is another way of loving. You can love without attachment, without desire. You can love without attachment to the objects of your love. You can love without fooling yourself that the things you love are indispensable either to you or to the world. Love is real only when you know that what you love must one day die."

"In your world everything is illusion," June said.

"No. Birth and death are real. They are the constants. All else is variable. In the rest you see what you want to see. According to the Hindu mystics there is a reality beyond all this. But I don't know. I would like to know some day."

I looked at my watch. Time was running out. June should be home soon, I thought, or Babu might misinterpret the whole thing.

I said, "Let's have something to eat. What will you have?"

"I am not very hungry. Order whatever you like."

"You used to like lobsters," I said grinning. She smiled back at me.

"Be careful. They must be very expensive here."

"They pay me pretty well for throwing people out of work."

I ordered for both of us. Then I went into the rest room and washed my hands. I looked at myself in the mirror. Where had all that I had just related gone? Somewhere in that black head it had been registered and corrected and stored. From some inaccessible storage bin it governed my life and I had no alternative but to obey its commands.

When I came back, June said, "Have you been able to follow that way of life?"

I had been afraid she would ask that.

"I had until I met you," I said. "It received a pretty bad beating at your hands. You don't know how hard I struggled before making love to you that evening we came from the beach. That night you had set off an avalanche that I had no means of stopping. It was lucky you left me. I was miserable when it happened, but I would have been completely bankrupt if you had not done so."

"Isn't it possible to make love and yet be detached?"

"It is possible, but it is very difficult. At times I tried that with you, but I usually failed."

"Have you overcome your attachment now?"

"I don't know. It'll perhaps take some more time. But it is too early to reckon up the damages to other people."

"How could you have damaged other people?"

"One never knows. Take your case. Would you have offered to marry Babu if you had not got disgusted with me at that very precise moment?"

"I was never *disgusted* with you."

"Maybe not. But you wanted to be of use and you wanted to feel that you were needed. And since you thought I didn't want you, you chose to be of use to Babu, even though it meant you had to sacrifice yourself."

She didn't say anything. We finished dinner and started for Boston. It was almost ten. On the way back we didn't talk much. I had come to Boston to help her but had only talked about myself. But she had calmed down considerably in the process. She had perhaps derived some new strength from the knowledge of my own struggle.

It was almost eleven when we reached my hotel. She came up with me and we had some coffee.

I stood near the window and watched the street lights below. June sat in the middle of the room and I knew that she was watching

146

me. She got up and came very near me. In a husky voice she said, "You are beautiful, Sindi, beautiful as a god. I don't think I can stop loving you."

I thought it was a parting comment and I smiled at her. Suddenly she stepped forward and clasping me around the neck she pressed her mouth against mine. She kissed me steadily and her heart beat against my chest. Her body was tense and slightly trembling. For a while I held back from her but I knew that she wanted me. Months of struggle to satisfy Babu's whims and innocence had left her depleted, and now she wanted a gesture of love from somebody she trusted. Was I to say no? I had come all the way to help her. That was perhaps all I could do for her.

I put my cup down and took her in my arms. I caressed her like a child and when I made love to her it was not in lust or passion but in a belief that I was helping her to find herself. It didn't strike me that she belonged to Babu and there were three—and not two—persons involved.

When she left she wore an almost benign expression on her face.

"I am sure I can stand by Babu now in whatever he does," she said.

After she was gone I read for a while. Then I went to sleep; I had to catch the early plane to New York.

In the middle of the night I was awakened by the ringing of the telephone. It was June. She was perturbed and sounded very upset.

"Babu is gone," she said.

"Yes?" I said. Over the next ten minutes she told me incoherently what had happened.

After leaving me, June had gone to Babu's flat and found him in a sullen mood. She had tried to cheer him up, but he lost his temper and asked her where she had been. She told him she had spent the evening with me. Babu sarcastically asked her if she had been sleeping with me. This made June angry, and she told him that as a matter of fact she had been sleeping with me and, what's more, she had been doing that for a year before she met him. At that Babu had suddenly grown pale. He had faltered for a while as if he were going to have a fit. Then he had called her a whore and hit her in the face. June had tried to explain the thing to him, but before she could finish he had left the flat and driven off blindly in his car.

147

In the end June said, "I've waited for him for four hours but he hasn't returned. I am getting worried, Sindi. Can you do something?"

I looked at my watch. It was four o'clock.

"There is nothing we can do except call the police. I'll ring them up and call you back."

I rang up the police and asked if a white convertible had been involved in an accident. I waited tensely while they checked. At last a voice said, "No, sir. There have been no accidents so far tonight." I gave them my telephone number, and asked them to ring me if anything turned up.

I told June there was nothing to worry about and that she should go home. I promised to stay on in Boston until Babu returned. Then I went back to sleep.

It must have been about eight o'clock when the telephone rang again. It was the police. They said they had discovered a white convertible, the driver was dead, and could I come to the morgue.

I went to the morgue as I have described earlier and identified Babu's body. The car, according to the police, had hit an overpass at high speed and rolled into a ditch. Later on I called June and gave her the news. I also cabled Babu's father in India.

I took leave from the company and stayed on in Boston for a week following Babu's death. There was little I could do to ease June's grief, but I wanted to be there in case she needed me. She continued to work on the theory that it helped her to forget. We usually spent the evenings at her house, just sitting together, saying nothing. I suppose there was nothing left to say, or it was so long and involved that we didn't know where to begin.

Once she looked at me accusingly and said, "Look, what your detachment has done."

I said nothing. The whole episode had left me baffled. All along I had acted out of greed, selfishness and vanity and had hurt nobody very much. When I had come close to gaining true detachment and had acted out of goodness, I had driven a man to his death.

I left June and went back to New York. In those next few days my knowledge of engineering was almost all I had left. In that world things didn't change without identifiable causes. You could depend upon a cam to operate a valve at the right time. And that, I must admit, was a great relief, considering the chaos I had been through. Occasionally, in my more pensive moments, I thought of Babu and I couldn't help feeling that I had lost a friend.

In a vague way I felt that something more was to come. I had a feeling that the state of my mind had not yet congealed. It had to go one stage further.

And then the next stage came. One afternoon in the labs, when I was in the middle of a difficult problem, it suddenly struck me that something had been knocked out of me. I just was not the same person any more. Babu's death had drained something out of me. It was my confidence in the world. At one blow most of what I had cherished in life was taken away. What I had considered beyond good and evil had produced evil on a gigantic scale; and what I had thought to be the remedy for pain had at one stroke created pain that was like a bombshell exploding under my nose. I felt as if there was nothing left that I could depend upon.

Babu had kicked out all my beliefs and disproved all my theories. I felt like a desert or like a vast field of naked oaks in winter time. I felt more alone and naked in the world than I had ever felt before.

I worked for another month. Then one morning while New York was flooded with spring I decided to move. America had taught me all she could and now it was time to leave. The feeling of my nakedness in the hands of existence grew with every passing day and a strong urge possessed me to once again roam the streets of the world. I didn't know where I would go or what the future held for me, but one thing was certain: my search had to continue. I had solved some of the questions life had posed for me; but many more remained to be solved.

I had an interview with the people at the United Nations. They asked me whether I wanted to work in the West or in the East. But that was beside the point. I only wanted a place where I could experiment with myself. I had many alternatives in the beginning; but ultimately I was left with two: I could go to Nigeria as a UN Consultant to the Government of Nigeria or I could try my luck in India. Both of them meant the same to me and for many days I could not make up my mind. Finally, one evening, sitting in a bar, I felt that I had to make a decision. The bartender was an old friend and I asked him what I should do. He took out a dime and flipped it high into the air and as it rang down on the counter he covered it with his hand.

"Heads for Nigeria," I said.

The coin showed tails. New Delhi.

14

GOING TO India brought a new kind of experience into my life. Earlier I had not cared much where I went. Now that my destination was decided, I looked forward to visiting the land of my ancestors with an interest I had not felt before. I spent whole evenings brooding over wisps of the culture my uncle and aunt had conjured up when I was a boy. They had fervently hoped they could give me a place to anchor on this lonely planet. Their hopes were misplaced, but the anecdotes I remembered did help me put some flesh on the skeletal outline of India which I had carried about in my head like a somnambulist's dream. I even bought a guide book on India and on weekends when I had nothing else to do I pored over its pages.

An even greater motivation was getting away from America. It meant escape from a bit of myself that appeared the most decayed. I thought of the departure as a process of walking up a ramp and a day later finding myself in an enchanted land where nobody recognised me and I could start life anew. Like many of my breed, I believed erroneously that I could escape from a part of myself by hopping from one land mass to another. I was like a river that hopes to leave its dead wood behind by taking an unexpected plunge over a steep precipice.

But I never fooled myself entirely. I had left England under exactly the same circumstances and enshrouded with similar reasoning. I convinced myself though that there was more than an even chance now that my life might work out in an unexpectedly happy manner. Some people made switches that altered their entire lives. It all depended on luck, and I had reached a plane of existence where I depended as much on luck as I did on careful choice and thoughtful planning. It was a flip of the coin.

I did not want to leave my company in the lurch, so I decided to wait until my project was finished. But I set in motion the necessary activity to clear my passage.

Getting a visa from the Government of India turned out to be an argument. It seemed they were not particularly interested in having foreigners settle permanently in their country. Some of the junior officials in the New York consulate openly discouraged me from pursuing my plans.

While my case dragged on, there were moments when I almost gave up. Finally, I was called for an interview with the consul general. He was a young person who talked like Sir Anthony Eden. He seemed sad and bored like the rest of his staff, and when he talked, rather than look at me he kept his gaze fixed on a portrait of Mahatma Gandhi on his desk.

It was a long inefficient session during which I told a string of white lies and committed myself to India's interests.

At one point he traced an ink stain on his desk blotter with his thumb-nail and asked, "You are not a Communist by any chance, are you?"

Like a well-catechized child I told him I had no political beliefs. That was the truth.

There were a few more inane questions and a few general queries about my parents and means of livelihood. Then, in a switch I never understood, he started talking about his days in England when he was studying at Oxford. While he talked his voice grew sadder and more beautiful until it sounded like poetry. He droned on for about fifteen minutes, then stopped abruptly and sat straight in his chair. He took a pen and signed my application hurriedly, as though he had suddenly remembered a forgotten engagement.

"Take this to the lady on the second floor, and she will give you the visa."

A thrill of joy spread through me when I stepped onto the street. To celebrate, I went into an ice-cream shop and ordered a huge banana split. While I ate it I wondered if it was my last banana split in America. I decided to play a record on the juke box, and just to please the fat girl behind the counter, I asked what she would like to hear. She wouldn't answer, but she giggled unaccountably while the record played. I chuckled along with her. It was likely that neither of us could have told the other what was funny. I decided to squander another dime and asked her again what she would like to hear. She gave me a title this time. I punched the number and had another bite of my banana split. When the song began the girl started giggling again. It was a popular tune:

> *If I ever love you.*
> *I am gonna' love you,*
> *All the way.*

I could not place it, but the song sounded familiar.

I asked the girl if she had any boy friends. That touched off another giggle. She said she had two, but she liked one of them the most because he was "clean-cut" and had a good mind. I didn't know what she meant by clean-cut. The song went on:

Who knows, who knows
Where the road will lead?
Only a fool can say.

That reminded me. "I'm going to India," I told the girl.

"Is that right? How wonderful!"

I patted the passport in my suit pocket and smiled behind her back, meeting her eyes in the mirror.

"Going home?" she asked.

"Yes," I lied, and then qualified it: "You might say that."

"Give me your address. I might write to you."

That was a likely story.

"I don't have an address yet, but you can write in care of the American Express in New Delhi."

The girl giggled again, presumably pleasuring at the wonderful blessing that was American Express. I paid her and left.

I took the subway to my apartment. Even the underground world of subway was celebrating the rites of spring. The air in the usually dirty, dark caverns tasted cleaner and lighter, as if the demigods of spring had swept it clean of stale cigarette smoke and body odours. Gaily dressed women transformed the waiting platforms into flower gardens. The dark, heavy garments of winter had been replaced overnight with bright cotton prints that clung to lithe bodies, spreading sensuously over every swell and contour. They hung about on the arms of their men or in little clusters by themselves, chattering and laughing, laughing, laughing. The female population of New York had come out in full force to formally and jointly approve the phenomenon of spring before it disappeared.

I felt so light-footed I could hardly stand in one place. I wanted to do a tap-dance I had learned in the dancing school in Nairobi. It was long ago, but I still remembered. But dancing was too conspicuous, so I walked up and down, humming the song I'd played in the ice-cream shop.

Taller than the tallest tree,
Deeper than the deep blue sea,
That's how it's going to be,
All the way.

A young woman stopped near me with a little boy dressed in blue hanging on to her hand. Her face was turned away, but I could tell by her hands that she was beautiful. I stepped back to admire her. She reminded me of June. Then I walked away. All that was behind me. It was spring in New York and before it died I would leave for India— where nobody knew me and spring was eternal. It was only a matter of days. Reassured, I moved towards the train as it screeched to a halt.

Even my apartment had been transformed. The landlady had been in and had made up the place with extra care. The bathroom smelt of Cleanzo and there was a bright yellow cover on the bed. There was a letter from June addressed in her girlish hand propped conspicuously on the mantelpiece against a black bust of Benjamin Franklin. The windows were open and my shirts shivered in the breeze.

I was hungry. I went to the kitchen and made myself a sandwich. God bless American Express and God bless A & P for providing such nicely sliced ham. Even if nothing else was remembered, progeny would applaud A & P for its contribution to twentieth century civilization. The Statue of Liberty was disconsolate in vain; it had got much more than was bargained for.

Halfway through the sandwich I remembered the letter and went to get it. It had no dateline and began abruptly.

'I have written this letter twice before, but each time, at the last moment, I lost courage. And what I am going to say calls for a measure of courage that I do not possess.'

My heart beat faster with premonition and skipped a few lines to a spot where the words flamed out of the blue writing paper.

'Sindi. I am carrying Babu's child and I don't know what to do.'

I put down the sandwich and wiped my hands on my trousers. Then I went back to the beginning of the letter and started again.

'I have written this letter twice before, but each time, at the last moment, I lost courage. And what I am going to say calls for a measure of courage that I do not possess. But as you said once, there is a kind of courage that comes with despair and I suppose this is what is happening to me. Sindi, I am carrying Babu's child and I don't know what to do. It is nearly four months now. He knew it when he went off that night but I can't blame him; it was my fault. I do not know what to do. I have not told mother yet. Actually, I have not told anybody; it

153

is such a horrible thing. I didn't tell you before because I didn't want you to get involved and feel as if you had to do something. I do not want you to do anything. I want you to be free of this terrible nightmare that I got myself into. It is just that I want to talk to somebody and you are the only one I can trust, and if I may use the word, love. I don't want you to worry. I am sure I'll find a way out.'

Her letter ended there. Then, as usual there was a post-script.

'P.S. I wonder if you are coming to Boston in the near future. I so much want to see you again and talk to you and touch you. Please let me know if you are coming.'

I folded the letter and put it back in the envelope, then tucked it away in my breast pocket as though it was a secret document that should not be left available to prying eyes. Methodically I gathered what remained of my sandwich and dropped it into a paper bag I kept by the stove for trash. I walked to the living room, and for a long while stood in the middle of the floor and stared at Benjamin Franklin's bust. Pregnant. Babu's baby. My thoughts were scrambled. I must have stood there for several minutes, maybe half an hour. Then a cacophony of querulous voices rose from below my window and I went over to see what was happening.

It was not much of a quarrel. A bunch of Negro boys stood in the middle of the street arguing about who was supposed to take credit for something that had happened. Periodically they fell silent and gazed up at a second floor balcony of an apartment house across the street. Then they would start talking simultaneously. A few minutes later a fat old lady shuffled out on the balcony like a bugler in a fancy Swiss clock. She shook a fist at them and cried, "Here, you goons!" Then she threw an old weathered softball at them and disappeared. The boys slapped their thighs, whooped and vanished around the corner. The street was silent, and in my mind the tune came back!

> *Who knows where*
> *The road will lead?*
> *Only a fool can say.*

The song had been familiar and now I realised why. It was the tune that had burst upon June and me in the cafe where I had met her to tell her of Babu's death.

Babu, you miserable, miserable fool, I thought. You stupid wretch, see what wretchedness your innocence has perpetrated. Had he been standing alive before me I could have strangled him with my bare hands there by my living room windows. Behind Babu lay the stupidity of his father and his sister and his entire civilisation. I hated everything that was Indian, as if the whole nation had conspired to debauch June. Angry and shocked, I paced the living room until it became oppressive and stifling. Then I locked the apartment and went out.

The spring was black with my hatred. It infested the sky-scrapers and hung over the city like a pall of infectious fallout. The gods of spring hid when my hatred roared through the merry streets like an unpropitiated ghost, a ghost of the past, stronger than the gods. And June had lied to me. Babu *had* been sleeping with her.

I threaded my way through the streets, unmindful of the crowds and laughter that surged around me. What I needed was to pass the time as quickly as possible and try to forget what I had come to know. Above all, I wanted to retrieve the tranquillity I had possessed before the letter came. The meagre quota of my happiness had been squandered away pathetically.

I hung around the Rockfeller Center, walking aimlessly, and later in the afternoon I went into Radio City Hall to sit down for a change. It was a Walt Disney movie and the hall was full of children. The movie was about a boy and his dog. The dog could read and play an accordion. He was a great delight for the children, stirring up lively little melodies every five minutes. I sat ensconced between two little girls who sat sedately, dangling their legs below them. Each had a huge box of popcorn in her lap as if she expected to be locked up in Radio City Hall for the rest of her life. They smiled self-consciously at me and occasionally passed objects to each other.

I forgot about June during the movie, but when intermission came my misery returned. Instead of chorus girls they had a magician to entertain the children. The little girls on each side of me stood up on their seats and squealed, but I could not get away from myself. I was intrigued with the necromancy of ghosts.

I took out June's letter and went over it again in the semi-darkness. "There is a kind of courage that comes with despair and I suppose that is what is happening to me." Was she desperate? She said she would find a way out. Perhaps she was just depressed at the time she wrote the letter. I read the postscript again. She wanted me to come and see her. I was willing to go, but I wondered how it would help. Could I suggest what she might do in her predicament? Should I marry her? I mulled it over some more and then decided I would go as soon as I could.

I didn't sleep well that night. Things have a way of bothering me much more at night. A couple of times I got up and switched on the light and read June's letter. Each reading conditioned me, and finally, near dawn, I dropped into a brief slumber.

When I got up, things were much brighter. It was a great relief to get back to the routine of the laboratory. I asked my project manager if there was any chance of my going to Boston in the near future. He told me I could go the next week. I dropped June a letter and told her I would come. I added briefly that I was surprised and sorry to hear of her difficulty but I didn't dwell upon it. I thought we could discuss it better when I saw her.

I had grown accustomed to the knowledge that June was pregnant. In many ways it was one more sad fact to be indexed in my little universe. As the week passed, the initial state of shock wore off and I was left only with a vague sense of gloom which was not very unlike my normal state of mind. Who could evade the randomness of existence? Not even June.

My anger for Babu remained. Only a few days before the letter I had persuaded myself that I was finally rid of him. But he had won even in his death. He still lived with me and grew larger every day in the belly of a girl that I once had loved with such strange passion. I pondered over these thoughts until my anger grew stifling. In a way, I looked forward to seeing June to find a release from my anger.

As it turned out, my visit to Boston had to be postponed for four days. Since it was a minor change it did not occur to me that I should inform June. I was surprised and felt a little guilty, when I received another letter from her.

'I waited for you the whole day today. Did you not say
you would come today? Mother had cooked a huge roast
for you and she was disappointed. Do come, Sindi. I
know I have no right to ask this of you, but please come—
for the sake of old times, if for nothing else.
'P.S. Mother says that she is saving a nice tender turkey
which she will cook for you when you come.'

I wanted to ring her up and tell her what had happened, but then it seemed pointless, since I would see her in two days.

15

NEW YORK had been warm and clear when we took off. But when the big jet thundered onto the Boston runaway it was raining heavily. Night had fallen and the dark was even more intense because of the overcast. Some incoming flights apparently had been diverted. The airport lobby seemed more empty and quieter than usual. Our flight must have been the only one to arrive in several hours. I collected my luggage and headed for the front entrance, passing concessions counter where the orange fountain gushed. I remembered Babu. Boston held many memories for me, vaguely sad ones now. The image of the bright orange fountain contrasted with the terrible irrevocableness of the past.

There were no cabs outside. As it always happened when it rains and when business is slow at the airport they had disappeared in the labyrinth of the city. I set my luggage down and leaned against the building. A car swung onto the drive and pulled up opposite me.

"You want a ride to the city?" It was a fellow passenger whose wife had come to pick him up. I grabbed my luggage and stuffed it in the back and climbed in.

On the way the man asked me if I was a student. I told him I had been until recently but now I was working. The driver's wife squirmed around on the front seat and asked me where I was from. I told her I was an Indian but had grown up in Kenya.

"Oh, how wonderful!" She was a well-built woman with dark hair and spectacles that made her look like a scholarly version of Elizabeth Taylor. Every now and then she patted herself in the middle of her chest as if she wanted to remind us how nice her figure was.

The man stopped the car under the hotel canopy and I got out and unloaded my luggage. When I closed the back the woman rolled down her window.

"We'll see you then," she said. They waved and drove off.

So they would see me, would they? That is the loneliness of our times, I thought as I rode up in the elevator. Strangers promise to see

157

you without even knowing your name. You are a king in a deck of kings, shuffled and reshuffled, meeting fifty-one similar kings but never saying anything sensible, never exchanging names.

When the bellboy had finished puttering around and left with his pittance I raised the window and surveyed the street nine storeys below. The rain was beginning to let up. I felt tired and decided to soak myself in a tub of hot water before calling June.

I thought of her while the water relaxed my muscles. How many times she had washed my back. I wondered what she was doing at the moment. Probably reading. Or listening to music and having a cup of hot chocolate. Was she still fond of chocolate, or had Babu altered her tastes? Maybe she was in bed. That would be the cosiest place on a rainy night. I slid down in the tub and the greenish water inched across my navel and flooded onto my chest. Long evenings together in my bed, warm, naked, limbs entwined. Love-making in all its beauty and fierceness. And then I remembered with vividness the spurting of my seed inside her and her joy at receiving it. I sat up and the water sloshed. Instead of Babu's child she could have been carrying mine. But I was more clever and took precautions. I didn't want to get involved. One didn't choose one's involvement, however. Wasn't Babu's child my own, in a way? Hadn't I driven her into his arms? The thought of marrying her crossed my mind again. What purpose would it serve, considering how far apart we had grown and my views against marriage? Then I thought I would wait and see if June had any such thing on her mind.

When I hurried out of the hotel to catch a cab the rain had slowed down. There were hardly any lights and the clouds hung thick and black over the city, giving it a desolate, weird look. It was almost ten o'clock and the streets were empty except for a few cars splashing through puddles of water.

June's home was dark and quiet like the rest of the city. It looked like a doll's house when the lights are out and the children gone to sleep. June and her mother were most likely in bed. I hated to wake them up but I wanted to see June as soon as possible. I rang the bell and it sounded unusually loud when it echoed through the house. I waited, wondering which of the two would come down.

When no one came I rang again and waited some more. Then I rang a third time. Waiting, no answer. I kept my thumb on the bell for several seconds, listening to it jangle through the downstairs rooms. I was almost ready to give up when a window on the first floor of the

158

neighbouring house clanged open and a rectangle of light shot into the darkness, forming a bright patch around me as if I was the accused, suddenly forced to face an invisible jury. The light dazzled me, and it was only when the hoarse voice croaked that I realised I had been spotlighted by an old woman in a nightcap.

"Can't you see the house is all shut up that you go on ringing like you owned the street!"

"Where is Mrs. Blyth?" I shouted back.

"How do I know where she is?" the woman grumbled. "I can't keep track of everybody on this street."

She seemed to have the street rather prominently on her mind.

"Isn't her daughter home?"

"She's dead!"

"What?"

"She died two days ago!" the woman repeated. She raised her voice against a roll of thunder.

There was something wrong somewhere. Was one of us confused? Then a slow, creeping emotion tainted with an unidentifiable fear began spreading through my mind.

"You must be mistaken," I said. The remark was more to myself than to the old woman in the upstairs window.

She started to close the window and I panicked. Leaping from the porch, I ran towards the low fence that separated the houses. "Don't go away yet!" I shouted. "Please! I have come a long way. She died?"

"Of course, she died! She had an abortion! They buried her today."

I sagged against the damp wood of the fence and wiped sweat and rain from my brow. There was nothing more to say.

The lady was still standing at the window, one hand on it as if she had been about to pull it down when she found me curious.

"You can sit on my porch till the rain stops, if you want to," she said finally.

She closed the window and the light went out. I was alone in the darkness again. Only the raindrops pranced about me, like a brigade of drummers. I stumbled back to the porch in the darkness and leaned against the wall while the wind lashed my face with rain. I stood there until I could see where I was going. Then I went to the front door and turned the knob. It was locked. I went around to the back. That door was locked, too, but I knew a kitchen window that could be opened

159

from the outside. The wood had swollen because of the rain and I had to pull hard to release the window from the frame. It creaked on its hinges when I swung it back and crawled inside.

I don't remember everything I did in June's house that night, but much of it is still painfully clear. At first I just walked aimlessly from room to room. Every object jumped at me with admonition. Once I raised my eyes to the mantelpiece in the living room and found myself looking straight into her eyes, the deep blue eyes that never ceased to love and wonder. After that I avoided photographs. I sat in a chair, then got up and wandered around some more. I was trembling and my throat was parched. I went into the kitchen and opened the icebox. The water bottles were full and I took one of them to the dining room.

I sat down in my usual chair and drank from the bottle. The cold water restored me a little but the dazed, nightmarish quality of the experience was still there, unrelieved and unreal.

The telephone rang. It burst through the quietness of the house like a charge of gunpowder and I started out of my chair. I went to the corner and stood over it, listening to the harsh ring, I had the unreasonable feeling that June was on the other end. Then it stopped.

It was after the phone stopped ringing that despair caught me by the throat and I started crying. I sat in the chair with my hands on my knees and cried. But it was no good. There was no relief.

After a while I went upstairs and wandered around in the dark, looking for the switches. I found the light in June's bedroom and switched it on. Her bed was unmade and seemed to exude a flickering warmth, like a body in which the heart has only recently ceased to beat. I moved about the room, examining it minutely. Her hairbrush lay in its usual place, the comb stuck in the bristles. At the base of the mirror a row of lipstick tubes stood like a formation of golden soldiers. Everything was waiting for her. But she would never come back. When I turned away from the dressing table I knew she would never again be back.

I knelt down by the bed with my face in her pillow. It smelled of her hair. I gathered the pillow under my head and wept again. She was dead and I didn't even see her before she died.

I must have remained there beside June's bed for a long time. Suddenly the doorbell rang. Startled, I got up and went down the stairs. A policeman stood on the porch. He was dressed in a blue raincoat, looking queerly like a ghost.

160

"Everything OK?" he asked, and peered beyond me into the living room.

"OK? Yes, I suppose so."

"The lady next door saw the lights and wanted us to check around."

"I see," I said as calmly as possible.

"Has anything happened? he asked. "Anything unusual, I mean?"

"I don't think so."

"The lady told me the people who live here are gone." He pushed me gently aside and went into the house. He peered into the living room, then turned and looked at me.

"You live here?"

"No. I'm a friend of the family," I wasn't crying any more but I felt terribly depressed.

The policeman unzipped his raincoat and pushed it back at the sides revealing the polished handle of his gun. He strolled down the hall and disappeared in the kitchen, then emerged and went up the stairs. I sat down on the threshold and waited. After a few minutes, he came back carrying June's pillow.

"Where is everybody?" he said.

"I don't know. Mrs. Blyth has gone somewhere and June, of course, was buried today."

"Today?"

"I mean yesterday." June was already more than two days dead.

He was silent for a while. He stood watching me while I peeled the darkness for a clue to the abominable absurdity of the world.

Then he spoke again, "How come this pillow is wet?" In some vague way he seemed to resent the fact.

"I'm afraid I've been crying into it," I said. "It's June's pillow, actually."

"Who are you? Are you a student?"

"I used to be. Now I'm working in New York."

"Have you got an identity card or a driver's licence?"

I took out my billfold and handed him my university card and my driver's licence. He squatted, and with a ballpoint wrote my name and licence number on a pad, then gave the cards back.

"Who's this girl, June, you're talking about?" he asked.

"She was a friend," I said. "She was going to have a baby and something went wrong, I guess."

The cop stood up and straightened his raincoat. He took out a

Viceroy and lighted it. Perhaps he, too, was a man of the world. "You taking care of things here?"

"No," I said. "I just came to see her. I didn't know she had died. The neighbours told me."

The policeman looked satisfied, then he said, "Do you need any help, sonny?"

He addressed me as if I were a juvenile delinquent or something. His attitude amused me and I couldn't fight back a slight smile.

"I guess I do," I said, "but I don't know in what way." I kept my eyes straight in front of me, as if I were a sage deciphering the dark hieroglyphs of the shadows.

"You sure you don't need any help?" He seemed insistent. Maybe I looked like I needed help.

"Perhaps I should just sit here and sort it out by myself, don't you think?"

"Well, then, good luck," the cop said. He zipped up his raincoat. "I hope everything works out all right, I think you're OK."

The remark surprised me. It had not occurred to me that I was being judged by anyone but myself.

He brushed past me onto the porch, then turned and said, "I'll see you then." His steps grated as he marched down the street, a rigorous member of the Boston Police force.

The rain had stopped and the sky was clearing. From the smell of the air I knew that dawn was not far off. In another hour it would be light.

All of a sudden, I wanted to get away from that house. I went to the kitchen and pulled the window shut and bolted it, then went to the front door, set its lock and pulled it shut behind me.

I went to the river and watched the dawn break over the dark waters. Inch by inch the sun climbed out of the womb of the universe. It reminded me of the morning I had sat on the rock overlooking the valley and experienced my first insight into the mystery of existence. But that was only half the lesson.

Detachment at that time had meant inaction. Now I had begun to see the fallacy in it. Detachment consisted of right action and not escape from it. The gods had set a heavy price to teach me just that.

The sight of the sun trajecting into the pathless void, certain of its oblivion at the end of the day, filled me with a measure of peace. There was assurance that the universe would click on, even though

Babu and June and their child were gone. I was the only one left who had the complete record.

Leisurely, I walked back to the hotel. The reception clerk turned on his seat and smiled knowingly at me.

"Must have been a long party, sir."

"Yes," I replied. "Very long." Then I gave him the name of the Catholic cemetery where I guessed June would have been buried and asked if he knew where it was. He knew, and he drew a map to show me how to get there.

The caretaker at the cemetery was not yet fully awake but he told me how to find the grave. It was green all around and very quiet. Clumps of daffodils stood around the graves shivering on their stalks as if they grew in dread of the dead below.

June's grave was situated between two evergreen trees on a knoll. The rain had beaten heavily on the grave and the mound of fresh earth had been eroded in places. A wreath of roses lay half buried in the mud, turned over on its tripod as if it had been kicked by some blasphemous passerby. I straightened the bent tripod and stood the wreath upright against the mound. A dirty, discoloured card attached to the tripod said the staff and management of Nantucket Mutual deeply mourned the death of their friend, June A. Blyth. I thought some other girl probably was already sitting at the grey desk that used to be June's. It doesn't take long to replace the dead.

For a while I stood near the grave, my hands in my pockets and my hair blowing in the morning breeze.

While I stood there the caretake ambled up to me. He was a short old man with a wrinkled leathery face and when he spoke I noticed that most of his teeth were missing.

"The storm really messes up these graves, don't it?"

"Yes," I said.

"Didja know her?" he said indicating the grave with his head. "The old lady said she was very young."

"Yes, she was very young."

He said it was funny how people died so young these days. Then he asked me what she had died of. His voice was monotonous without any undertones of inquisitiveness. He was just having an early morning chat with a stranger.

"She was going to have a baby and something went wrong."

The caretaker coughed and wiped his mouth on his sleeve. He looked me up and down as if he had just discovered me.

163

"I bet you are feelin' pretty miserable." I wondered if he had mistaken me for June's husband.

I said, "I was for a while. The dead teach you how to overcome their death, though."

"Yeah?" he said wiping his mouth again with the back of his hand.

"I mean you learn something when other people die. Otherwise, how could you ever get used to their absence?"

"I guess you are right. Maybe you've got to get used to watching these graves dug day after day. You mustn't let them get you down."

I wondered if he was speaking to me or talking to himself. He waved towards the acres of grass.

"Once they get you down you are no good for nothing else, are you now?"

He looked at me as if my view was very important in this matter. I said I supposed so.

"You've got to go on behavin' like folks never died."

A multi-coloured pebble caught my eye near the grave. I stooped and picked it up.

"What d'ya say?"

I turned the pebble in my hand and decided to keep it.

"You are right. You have got to go on acting as if folks never died." After a pause I added,

"And you have got to stop being careless."

"Yeah?"

"You must not be careless." I repeated.

"Things have no meaning if they are not on time."

"Would you like a cup of coffee?" the caretaker said suddenly, coughing again.

"No, thanks. I had better be going."

That spring in New York I wandered about on the chequer-board of despair and hope. For the first time I became aware of the despair that had so long enveloped my being like a fish is surrounded by water. And, like a fish, I had always been unaware of it. I saw myself as I had always been. An uprooted young man living in the latter half of the twentieth century who had become detached from everything except himself. Where Kathy and Anna had taught me to be detached from others, June's death finally broke my attachment to myself. It was here that my hope lay.

I worked in New York for a few more weeks, just enough to finish the project I had started. As it had happened after Babu's death the laboratory provided me a sanctuary where I could forget my conflicts, at least at the conscious level. But in the inner recesses of my mind the trial went on. Each day the judges met and examined the witnesses. My parents, my uncle, my lovers, Babu and June, their parents, and finally myself, one by one all were called by the invisible judges and asked to give their evidence. Under normal conditions this would have been painful but after the shock of June's death it came as a great therapeutic process. I felt as if some indefatigable surgeon was cleaning up my soul with the sharp edge of his scalpel.

In my spare time I never left the apartment except to buy food or go to the laundry. When I did go out I walked about the streets lost within myself unseeing and unheeding while the scalpel continued to move from chamber to chamber and tissue to tissue cutting out much that was rotting and disembowelling cells which had never been seen before. It was an awesome sight.

In short I was seized with the problem of once again putting together all that had happened to me and coming to grips with life. For twenty years I had moved whichever way life had led me. I had learnt much on the way. I had learnt to be detached from the world, but not from myself. That is when the fatal error was made that ultimately led to Babu's death and then to June's death.

June's memory lingered with me like an incurable ulcer. Occasionally, I would see a woman who resembled June in some way and I would become painfully aware of all that she had meant to me. I also developed the habit of going down to the river and thinking about her while watching the boats. Her memories might have been less painful if I had talked with someone about her, but as usual, I had no friends.

Wouldn't Babu still be living if I had not surrendered my body to June that night we went out for a ride? I thought I was acting out of detachment but was it not merely a desire to prove that I still held the key to June's happiness?

I had presumed that I could extricate her from the web of her own actions; that I could make her happy by simply standing still and letting her use me whichever way she wished. Nothing could have been farther from the idea of detachment. That was a fatal presumption.

And if Babu had not killed himself June would still be living. It had all been a tremendous illusion that had led me to this destruction.

I was relieved when I finally submitted my paper. It was well received and my project manager told me I might get patent rights on the design if I remained in America. He urged me to stay, but I had no desire to change my mind. At last, one warm morning, while spring turned to summer, I left for India.

16

IT WAS a usual summer morning in New Delhi and I had been in India for a whole year. I thought of the previous summer as I sipped my coffee, staring out of the large filthy windows. It was good; the new peon really knew how to make coffee. The sun was high in the sky. One could almost see the waves of hot air moving up along the brick walls. The street was black with men, scurrying back and forth like a million ants. In the middle of it about a dozen men heaved at a concrete pole of huge dimensions.

They sang as they pulled and their dark muscular bodies glistened with sweat. And at the end of the day they would get two rupees or perhaps three. Mr. Khemka, it was said, made thirty thousand a day. The pole was very nearly off the cart. The men paused for a while, breathing deeply and wiping the sweat from their eyes Then, as if moved by an unseen hand, they heaved in unison yelling loud enough to turn heads. The pole tottered uneasily on the edge of the cart and then fell to the pavement.

It was a sad sight. The workers' clothes were falling off in rags and sweat poured off their backs as if they had just had a shower. What was the point in all those big men like Mr. Khemka talking about God and pain so long as half-naked men had to wrestle with a beastly mass of concrete under a scorching sun? And all for three rupees a day.

These are my people, I thought. And yet I moved among them as if I were a stranger. I wasn't alone. All of us who worked in Mr. Khemka's office or went to his parties, or sent him our daugher's wedding card were strangers. None of us knew what ugly brown men sang about as they heaved concrete poles off haggard old carts. And Mr. Khemka wanted to teach me about life.

He wouldn't be coming to the office today, I thought with satisfaction. They never came to the office on Saturdays. One could look forward to a day of peace.

But the peace of the morning was shattered when Mr. Ghosh dashed in frantically with two other men. "Good morning", he said, and pushed a paper under my nose. It bore a large seal and seemed to be from some big official in the government. It said something to the effect that we were ordered to present all the business documents desired by the representatives of the Income Tax Department.

"Well ?" I said looking up.

"I am sorry." Mr. Ghosh said with an ironic smile. "I will have to seal your books of business."

"What books of business ?" I said in honest bewilderment.

"Let's be frank, Mr. Oberoi, like two intelligent men of business. You know exactly what I mean."

"But I don't. All I have is this," I said pulling out the single drawer in my table. "Do you see any books of business here ?" I asked irritably. All the clerks were stealthily glancing at us from the corner of their eyes. Apparently they were enjoying the fun.

"Am I right in assuming that you are the senior most person in the office at this time?" Mr. Ghosh said in his best lawyerly manner.

"I suppose I am," I said looking at the row of clerks whom I presided over.

"Then I have to request you to call your chief accountant."

"We don't have a chief accountant. We have just one accountant and he is hard of hearing."

"Well, call him, please," Mr. Ghosh said in his most courteous tone.

I looked at him and then at the order in my hand. After all I had no reason not to call the accountant. I shouted across the room at Mr. Jain who pretended to be our accountant. I pitied the poor old man as he asthmatically shuffled across the hall.

I gave him the order. He was quiet for a little while as if stunned into silence. Then he visibly started trembling and stuttering.

Mr. Ghosh looked quite satisfied with his reactions.

"Now Mr. Jain, if you would be kind enough to show us the business documents, we would proceed with the job," he said patronisingly.

167

"But I can't. Sethji is not here."

"Never mind the Sethji," one of Mr. Ghosh's companions broke in suddenly and fell silent equally suddenly when Ghosh looked at him disapprovingly.

"Show us the books, Mr. Jain." Ghosh said. "Let us not waste any more time."

"I will, if Mr. Oberoi orders me to," Mr. Jain said, I hated to be dragged into the mess once again.

"What have I got to do with it?" I said irritably.

"You are the senior most person here," Jain replied. He seemed to have shed a bit of his original fright.

"Show them the books, for God's sake and be done with it," I snapped. I was getting tired of the whole business.

Ghosh sat at my table and ordered the other two about. Their bustle was quite a thing to see. They rushed about the place like gigantic beetles sealing everything they could lay their hands on. Now and then Ghosh turned around and smiled at me like a prince. I ignored him. Actually I did not quite know how I was supposed to behave. The whole thing was so novel and unexpected.

"What is it all about, Mr. Ghosh?" I asked tentatively after some time.

"What do you think it is all about?" he replied, his eyes twinkling behind the thick lenses.

"Well, I wouldn't ask you if I knew, would I?"

"Mr Khemka has been swindling the government for ten years and we have caught up with him now, that's what it is all about."

"What makes you so sure?"

"I have worked here myself. I know his racket inside out."

"I see. What do you propose to do next?"

"Lock him up for one thing."

"You are very powerful, are you?"

"I carry the power of the state," Ghosh replied pompously.

I thought of telephoning Mr. Khemka to brief him on what was afoot. On second thoughts, however, I decided in favour of seeing him in person.

"I suppose I am free to go, Mr. Ghosh, or am I...?"

As I went downstairs, Mr. Jain came scurrying after me.

"Don't leave me alone with these people, Sahib," he begged with folded hands.

He had never called me Sahib before.

168

"Why? What is bothering you?"

"They may take me to prison." To my astonishment he was weeping.

"Well? So what? It won't be any worse than here. And then it is a professional risk so far as you are concerned, isn't it?" Anger had made me cruel.

Jain's weeping turned into sobs.

"Don't worry," I said relenting a bit. "They haven't got a warrant."

I rushed down the stairs, my coat flying behind me, and left the place.

I was fully awake by now. There was no doubt that something serious was afoot about which Mr. Khemka had to be informed. He was most likely to be at the house at that hour of the day.

Mr. Khemka had just finished his prayers and was in the middle of a prodigious yawn when I was ushered in.

"The income tax people are here," I said when he had finished.

Mr. Khemka jumped up from his cushion as if it were on fire. His immediate response was amusing.

"Where?" he cried in a slow, shrieking whisper.

"In the office."

"And what are you doing here?" he shouted, his forehead beginning to roll up recording his rising anger.

"They kicked me out. What could I do in the office anyway."

"You fool, you fool," he moaned in impotent rage, "They might seal everything, don't you see?"

"That is exactly what they are doing right now," I said and for some reason I couldn't help laughing.

My words had the effect of a thunderbolt. Blood drained out of Mr. Khemka's face and all of a sudden he looked very old.

"Oh, God," he groaned sitting down on the low divan. He pressed his hands to his temples and his eyes were hidden from me. On the left side of his face the little finger twitched like a lizard's torn tail.

He was silent for a long time and except for the twitching finger, very still. Finally, he looked up. I thought he had calmed down, but I was wrong.

Suddenly he barked at me. "Why didn't you bribe them, you fool?"

"What ?" I asked somewhat puzzled.

"I said why didn't you bribe them ?" His temper was rising.

169

"I am afraid I didn't think of it."

"I know. That is just what is to be expected from a fool like you. I curse the day I set my eyes on you," he said in a sudden fit of repulsion.

"I'm sorry," I said and then I began to laugh. It was a kind of laughter that I get when somebody is being thoroughly ridiculous. The more I tried to control myself the more I laughed. Mr. Khemka looked at me in complete bewilderment. I don't think he had ever seen one of his employees behave like this. Tears of laughter rolled down my cheeks. I was pretty nearly getting hysterical and I thought the best thing would be to go away. I turned towards the door and ran into Sheila. She looked at me, then at her father, then again at me and began to smile though she looked a little puzzled.

"What is the matter?" she said.

By now my laughter was well under control.

"The income tax people have sealed the office," I said.

The smile faded from her eyes and she turned pale. For a moment she stared at her toes. Then suddenly she put her arms around her father. To my great astonishment, she began to cry.

I tried to think of something nice to say but nothing came to my mind. I didn't feel like laughing anymore. Things seemed much bigger than I had thought.

Hurriedly, I left the room. I crossed the dining room and then the living room. Everything was in order and very quiet. Babu smiled from his usual niche on the mantelpiece. Shiva danced away his crazy dance. Nothing had changed and yet the peace of the day had been shattered.

Outside, the wind shook dead leaves from trees, mingled them with dust and spread them over the pavements of Delhi. It was already autumn. I thought the trees would soon be bare. Autumns in India are not as beautiful as in America. As a matter of fact they are quite unpleasant.

I got into the taxi and drove away. Just as I came out of the house, a black car turned into the drive. It came to me as a shock for it belonged to the police.

I went home; there was no point in going back to the office. There was no point in going home either, but there was nowhere else to go.

The day dragged on. The afternoon was hot and my little flat got stoked up like an oven. I lay on my bed half naked flipping

170

through a colourless history of the Moghul empire. My cook tried to draw me into conversation but I told him I wasn't interested, so he went back to the book of mythology I had bought for him a month before.

In the middle of the afternoon the electricity went off and the fans came to a standstill. I opened the windows but there was no breeze. I was dazed with heat. It was my second summer in India but I had not yet got used to it. I sat on the bed, naked to the waist, staring out of the window. Except for a sweeper's baby who cried under the meagre shade of a boundary wall, the street was empty. Sweat poured down my forehead and into my eyes. Little streams started in my armpits tickling me as they rolled down my sides. The sky was light grey, almost white with heat.

The child's wailing became hoarse and then finally ceased and all of a sudden it was very quiet. And then it struck me that I was waiting for something. It seemed that I had never been to Mr. Khemka's office and that I would never go there again. It seemed that I had never done anything in my life except wait on that narrow bed. The room dissolved in the heat and I was sitting in the middle of a desert waiting for a prophet. I suppose it was just a hallucination of my mind under the heat but at the moment it all seemed very real.

Towards the evening I became calmer. I wondered what was happening to Mr. Khemka. Perhaps I should phone him but to do that I would have had to walk up to the market. And it was still too hot for that. Poor Sheila, she must be suffering a lot.

I had a drink and then another. But my depression only worsened. I didn't even answer when the cook came in and said a Memsahib wanted to see me. And when Sheila walked in, I didn't feel surprised. Perhaps that's what I had waited for all day.

She looked badly pulled down with her eyes swollen to twice their normal size with crying.

"You are drinking?" she said.

"It looks like that, doesn't it? Sit down." She sat down on the edge of the chair.

"How is Mr. Khemka?"

"They have taken him away," she said, her lips trembling a little.

"Who have taken him away?"

"The police. But he will be back tomorrow," she said, vainly trying to sound optimistic through her tears.

"What is the charge?"

"Evasion of income tax and embezzlement and a few others."

"Looks pretty bad," I said irrelevantly.

"Don't say that. It makes my heart sink." She was on the brink of crying.

I smoked a cigarette and then made myself another drink. She had her back to me as I poured the drink. She was slightly built with narrow shoulders. I noticed again how elegant she was.

"What are you going to do?" I said sitting down.

"I don't know. Father called his lawyer before going. He must be working on it."

"Is he guilty?"

"Yes."

"What did he do?"

"I don't know the details. He probably maintained two books and paid income tax on fictitious accounts."

"But surely he didn't keep those books in his office?" I said.

"He kept the real ones at home but the police have got them now. They ransacked the house this morning."

"Serves him right," I said.

Although it was still light outside, the room had darkened. I couldn't see her face. The crook, I thought, the mean little crook who had to steal money in spite of the millions he had. This was Indian business. So far one had only heard of it, but now it was real. And all along I had been a part of it.

"Serves him right," I said with increasing bitterness.

She didn't say anything. Then her whole body began to shake and I knew that she was struggling to keep down her weeping.

As I have said earlier, the sight of anybody weeping always gives me a bad feeling in the stomach. I tried to look away but I couldn't forget the little body trembling two yards from me.

"I am sorry," I said. But she didn't seem to be listening. I didn't quite know what else to do for her. I had no emotion, or money, or sympathy. What could I give her? Yet I felt sorry for her.

"I am sorry," I repeated.

"Don't bother," she seemed to say through her tears. I went up to her and put my arm around her shoulders.

"I am sorry, Sheila. I really am." •

She stiffened for a moment. And then she relaxed. She turned a little towards me and suddenly broke down with loud, irrepressible

172

sobs. She put her arms around my middle and pressed her face against my stomach.

"Oh, what am I to do, Sindi?" she groaned pausing for breath between words, "I'll be left all alone when they take him away. I will be left all *alone*."

I patted her head and her back awkwardly in a gesture of consolation.

When she had calmed down, I said, "Isn't there some way of saving him?"

"There is one way," she said. Then she shifted uneasily in her seat and added, "That is why I came to see you."

I waited for her to continue. I expected her to describe some complicated legal tangle in which she wanted my help. But she had something much simpler in mind. She cleared her throat. "I came to beg something of you," she said, then looked at her feet. I waited. I had begun to feel a bit like God.

"I came to ask you to tell the police that you were the one responsible for the whole thing."

"What?" I asked slightly puzzled.

She repeated what she had said before.

"But, how can I? I don't even know what it is all about."

"You don't have to know that. I'll manage it."

"Very kind of you," I said.

She kept quiet, still staring at her toes.

"Who put this into your head?" I asked.

"Nobody," she said, without looking up.

"Does your father know about it?"

"No, but I can persuade him."

"I'm sure you can," I said, laughing.

"Would you do it?" she said after a while.

"It would mean that I go to prison instead of him."

"It may." She avoided my eyes.

Suddenly I was angry. I got up and grabbed her shoulders and shook her.

"Don't just sit there and talk to me like that! Tell me, would I go to prison or not?"

She looked up at me aghast, her eyes opening wide with horror.

"Tell me the truth!"

"But, I don't know," she said breaking into sobs once again, "I don't know."

173

I let her go and went over to the window. My anger had subsided—it lay within me and not in anything that she had said. She had offered me a bad choice.

Behind me I was aware of her getting up and moving about the room. I heard the click of her handbag and then she was gone. I saw her once again in the street as she got into the car. Then she drove away.

After she was gone I had dinner and almost immediately went to sleep. I rested uncomfortably for only a few hours (my servant told me that I had been talking in my sleep). Then I woke up. It was pitch dark and very quiet except for the monotonous hum of the fan. My pillow was wet with sweat. As soon as I was awake, Sheila's request came back to me as a painful incident that I had just managed to tuck away at the time of going to sleep. For a long while I sat in bed thinking confusedly of the day's events. Then I got up and went out on the terrace. It was four o'clock. I put my hands on the banister and stared across the unbuilt plot that lay behind my house. The moon was still new. Except for the twinkling of a few lights, darkness lay upon the city like a burden of cosmic guilt.

I got dressed and left the house. I needed time to think this over. For the next two hours I roamed aimlessly through the deserted streets. Gusts of warm wind blew through the night. Occasionally I met a chowkidar or a policeman. They looked me over witth suspicion, then lost interest when they got a closer look at my clothes.

My footfalls echoed in the streets. I had a funny feeling that I was walking back into my past. It seemed only yesterday that I had driven to Mr. Khemka's house that summer evening. In the stagnant deadness of Mr. Khemka's world I had the feeling that I was settling down. In truth it had only been a change of theatre from America; the show had remained unchanged. I had met new people with new vanities. They merely had different ways of squeezing happiness out of the mad world. And they suffered differently.

I had reached Connaught Place. Barred shops waited blind-folded under the surveillance of their gaudy neon signs. I walked around the huge circle like a sleep walker in an amphitheatre. And as I walked I read aloud every signboard as though I had just learned to read. They all sounded rich and luxurious. I wondered if they all kept two books like Mr. Khemka.

Mr. Khemka, man of the world, municipal councillor, chairman of many committees, dynamic entrepreneur, master of ceremonies, darling of the astrologers, owner of a growing empire. Now I knew how the empire grew. Now I knew what people like Jain and me and Muthu had been slogging for: just so that Mr. Khemka could sit back and write his two books of accounts.

A tonga emerged from one of the side streets. The driver asked me if I wanted to go somewhere. I said I didn't but he continued to follow me. The rhythmic beat of the horse's hoofs on the asphalt sounded live and grotesque. At last, tired, I offered the driver a cigarette. While we smoked he kept asking me if I wanted to go somewhere. Then he started to talk about the misery of tonga drivers. I wasn't listening but I was glad he had ceased talking of going somewhere. He would probably have continued all night if a policeman had not appeared and told him to move on.

"You are not supposed to park here," the policeman said half-heartedly. The tonga driver bowed to him obsequiously. He turned his horse around and drove off.

"Are you looking for something, sir?" the policeman asked me.

"Yes," I said. "Have you seen God?"

The policeman must have thought I was nuts. He walked away without looking back.

I did not feel like walking anymore. The policeman had shattered the spell. I wanted to sit down quietly for a while and give Sheila's request a final thought before I told her my decision. I entered an inner garden and sat down on a bench. There are no lovers in Indian gardens. Only little heaps of humanity lay here and there, trying to snatch a few hours' sleep before sunrise.

I suppose I was expected to have reasons for refusing to help Mr. Khemka out. I had only one: Mr. Khemka had to suffer for his own actions. In the past I had tried to put the consequences of my actions on others, or presumed to take over their actions as my own. Both had boomeranged. In the end, both had done more harm than good.

A taxi whizzed past me, piled high with luggage. The morning train had apparently arrived. The sky in the east was greying after the night's mourning. I got up and walked home.

I met old men coming out for a walk. I suppose, like Mr. Khemka they would all have wanted to teach me about life. Did they have the answers I was looking for? I doubted it. I suspected they kept two books like Mr. Khemka—one for their neighbours, the other for God. At least I could claim the uniqueness of having just one book. The thought made me smile to myself.

I stopped at a chemist's shop and called Sheila, but there was no reply. I decided to go over personally to their house and tell her that my answer was no.

17

MR. KHEMKA's house had the typical look of a rich man's house at dawn. The night chowkidar had gone, but none of the morning staff had yet taken his place. The outer gate stood open and unwatched; perhaps nobody was anymore interested in guarding the citadel. Everything was still and very quiet except for the front door which creaked desolately on a loose hinge in the morning breeze.

None of the servants had yet come in from their quarters. Even the little boy who had opened the door for me had disappeared. The air-conditioner was not working in the living room but it was not warm yet. I sat down on the huge divan and yawned. I was physically exhausted by the night's wanderings, and I stretched myself on the divan to rest my limbs a little. Presently I fell asleep.

When I woke up it was nearly eleven. The house seemed as quiet as before but somebody had put a pillow under my head and removed my shoes to make me more comfortable. The heavy raw-silk curtains were drawn, cutting off the blinding light of summer and the air-conditioner was running. Altogether, I felt nice and comfortable. Since there was nobody around me, I decided that everybody was still in bed and turned over to go back to sleep. But then I heard the tinkling of plates and cutlery and I realised that there were people in the dining room.

I got up and lit a cigarette. My limbs still ached, but I was feeling much better. I looked around for my shoes but they were nowhere to be seen. Ultimately I gave up and walked over to the dining room in my socks.

Sheila and her father sat at one end of the dining table with huge glasses of orange juice in front of them. Mr. Khemka was reading the

176

newspaper, Sheila sat forlornly in her silent Buddha position, her immaculate hands folded in her lap. A stranger would have thought that they were worshipping the orange juice before drinking it down.

Neither of them took notice of me as I came in. It might partly have been due to the fact that I had only my socks on and I made very little noise while walking.

"Do you know where my shoes are?" I enquired tentatively from Sheila.

She looked up from her orange juice and I noticed that her eyes were red and swollen with crying.

"I put them under the divan. You looked uncomfortable in them."

"And I suppose you gave me the pillow, too."

"Yes. Why?"

"Nothing. It was awfully nice of you."

After this we were silent for a while until Mr. Khemka put down his paper and reached for the orange juice. Our eyes met.

"Good morning, sir," I said.

"Good morning." The reply was curt. He didn't seem to be on speaking terms with either me or his daughter.

A servant came and laid another place for me. Then he brought in an exactly identical glass of orange juice and put it in front of me.

The juice was nicely chilled and I enjoyed its feel as it trickled down my gullet.

"Nice juice," I remarked casually, carefully modulating my words. But immediately afterwards I knew what a foolish remark it was. As might have been expected, nobody took any notice of it.

After a while I ventured again.

"How are things?" I said addressing the air space between Sheila and Mr. Khemka.

"What things?" Mr. Khemka asked, putting down his glass.

"I mean things about your business."

"How do you expect them to be after the mess you have created?"

"I am sorry, but I don't know what you mean by the mess I have created. I don't know how anybody could have handled it differently."

"Oh, you could have bribed them or asked them to come again or some such thing. Surely something could have been done to hold them off for a day or two."

"Even if I could, what purpose would it have served?"

"What purpose would it have served?" Mr. Khemka sneered. His eyebrows reached high in his forehead.

"What purpose would it have served!" he exclaimed, as if he was incredulous of my stupidity. "It would have made all the difference in the world! I could have had the accounts straightened out before they were seized and I could have contacted just the right man in the government. And you ask me what purpose it would have served."

"Do you really believe that?" I asked him.

"Of course, I do."

"But don't you see they are out to get you? They've been working on you for more than a year now. Do you think you could have got away just by contacting the right person or changing your books of accounts overnight?"

"You don't know the influence of my contacts. They could have got us out of any difficulty."

"But why did you get into trouble in the first place? Why did you have to keep two books of accounts?"

Mr. Khemka smiled once again, his eyes reflecting the low opinion he held of my business judgement.

"I did it because everybody does it. You can't run a business these days without doing these things."

"I suppose you wanted to evade income tax?"

"Everybody does it," he said again. "What can the government expect if it stupidly goes on increasing taxes. It is part of the game."

"But a game has rules, Mr. Khemka. You can't label every dirty thing you do as part of the game."

"This is not a dirty thing," he exclaimed with emphasis, his temper beginning to rise again. "Were it not for that scoundrel Ghosh nobody would have ever known about it."

"A dirty thing is dirty whether somebody knows about it or not," Sheila said mildly, as if she were making a general point.

Mr. Khemka looked at her in surprise and blinked his eyes behind the thick rimmed spectacles.

"So, you too are turning against me?" he said.

Sheila looked even more uncomfortable than before but she kept quiet.

"Nobody is turning against you, Mr. Khemka, except of course the government. And they have every right to do so. You owe them such a lot of money, you know?"

I had hoped he would appreciate the joke. He only looked about himself dreamily.

178

"Had it not been for that man Ghosh, nobody would have known about it," he repeated bitterly.

"Why did he turn against you anyway?" I asked.

There was long silence. Mr. Khemka picked up his orange juice and put it to his mouth but he did not seem to be drinking. Finally he put it down. When he did not speak for a long time, Sheila said,

"Father sacked Mr. Ghosh two years ago."

"I sacked him because he was inefficient and a liar," Mr. Khemka growled.

"I don't know how efficient he was, father, but you certainly did not sack him for that. He was sacked for things he did not do. And then you refused to pay him for the whole month that he had already worked for you."

"No wonder he is out to get you," I said.

"The man who can get me is not born yet. People are foolish if they think they can get me as easily as that."

He said this with such childish pomposity that I couldn't help chuckling a little. This infuriated him all the more.

"Instead of feeling ashamed of your actions you have the cheek to laugh at what I say. It is shameful."

He had said this earlier, but this time he made me a little angry. I stopped grinning and turned to my juice. But he went on working himself into a self-righteous anger.

"Since you started with me I have had nothing but trouble. I wanted to be nice to you because you were Babu's friend. But you have only brought ruin on me. And now you laugh at me! You ought to be ashamed of yourself!"

"I am ashamed of myself, Mr. Khemka. But for different reasons. I am ashamed of having associated myself with you."

Sheila adjusted her sari uncomfortably and reversed the position of her hands. Without looking up she said,

"What has happened, has happened. Where is the point in quarrelling among ourselves?"

Mr. Khemka glared at her as if he disapproved of her speaking at all. Then, ignoring her remark, he went on.

"So you are ashamed of associating yourself with me, are you? Where would you be if I had not given you this job?"

That set me chuckling again.

"Where would I be? I don't know. I would probably be out on the streets pushing your loads from a factory or may be I would be

179

designing aeroplanes. I would have preferred either to being a part of your racket."

"I see," he said and picked up his paper, but I knew he was not reading.

"Has it come out in the papers yet?"

"No." Sheila said, "We are trying to keep it out."

"I suppose Mr. Khemka has contacts there also."

Mr. Khemka threw the paper on the floor. He put his hands on the table and I noticed that the little finger was twitching again, perhaps he wanted to slap me.

"I have contacts everywhere and you might like to know that they are not as ungrateful as you. You ought to be ashamed of yourself."

Now I was very angry. I said,

"It is not I who should be ashamed, Mr. Khemka, but you yourself. I have only been one of your victims. It is you who have swindled those miserable wretches in rags who push carts on your streets and die at twenty-five. It is you who have been telling lies and fabricating documents just so that you could air-condition this ostentatious house and throw gigantic parties for the horde of jackals who masquerade as your friends."

Sheila shifted uneasily in her seat. Mr. Khemka raised his hand as if to interrupt me but I raised my voice and continued.

"And don't forget you are one of them."

"Sindi!" Sheila cried, half rising from her chair.

Mr. Khemka's face was dark with rage but when he spoke his voice was calm and steady.

"People who don't have money are always envious of those who do. There is nothing wrong in making money and, mind you, only clever people can make money. Anyway in my case, I have worked hard just so that my children can live in comfort. I have... ."

"Is that why you drove your son to death by threatening to disinherit him?"

Mr. Khemka did not answer me. Instead, he said,

"You are crooked like the rest of us, Sindi, except that you are a little worse. You are an ungrateful upstart."

"What do you want me to be grateful for, Mr. Khemka?" I watched a ray of sunlight split into a rainbow through the cut-glass tumbler.

"Your heartlessness drove the only person I ever loved to death. You have prostituted my ability for a whole year for your diabolical

180

aims. And now you want me to go to prison for you. Is this what you want me to be grateful for?"

"I am not asking you to go to prison for me! The man who can send me to prison is not born yet. I just want you to admit your faults."

"But why? It was *not* my fault. I am not afraid of going to prison but this time it is your turn. I have sinned, and God knows, I have paid heavily for them. This time it is your name that is being called. It is you who must answer. That is the only hope of salvation you have left."

Mr. Khemka looked at me with mock detachment and smiled, his lips twisted with bitter sarcasm. He spoke slowly and deliberately.

"I may need advice but it is not from you, Mr. Oberoi—not from you of all people. Let us not forget what we are."

That is what Babu had said once. I couldn't help smiling at the coincidence. I wasn't trying to advise him anymore than I had advised Babu.

"I am not forgetting what I am. On the contrary, I am saying these things only because of what I am. We have both made a mess of our lives—and other people's lives. But I have learnt a thing or two while you are too vain—or too ignorant—to learn. You must stay out in the wilderness and howl into the night."

Mr. Khemka was mad with frustration and rage. He looked as if he wanted to say so many things at once that he did not know what to say first. Ultimately he said just one thing.

"I order you to get out of my house!" He shouted in a loud rasping voice that shook with rage. "I order you to get out of my house and never step in here again."

I knew that the time of our parting had come. The thought made me a little sad. I looked at Sheila but she wouldn't lift her eyes to meet mine. I put down my napkin and got up. A ponderous hush seemed to fall over the house like an enormous blanket. I said,

"I'll go. Mr. Khemka. But you can't get rid of your sins by just turning me out. They will stalk you from every street corner just as they have stalked me. We think we leave our actions behind, but the past is never dead. Time has a way of exacting its toll and the more you try to hold out, the heavier the toll is. How long can your contacts stand against the ravages of the desert that is within you? You... ."

Before I could finish Mr. Khemka got up and stamped out of the room. And with his departure I realised the folly of my having got into

181

an argument with him. Everything was quiet once again except for the steady hum of the air-conditioner. I poured myself a cup of coffee and looked at Sheila.

"You are crying again," I said smiling.

"How could you be so heartless?"

"I am heartless, am I? Just because I told him what he is?"

"It is easy to tell others what they are, Sindi. I wish people would help each other, too."

"I have told you why I wouldn't get involved into his mess. What other kind of help do you expect of me?"

"I don't know. I wish you had been kinder to him."

"What purpose would it have served, Sheila? Sooner or later he has to face up to what he is."

"But you didn't have to tell him to his face."

"I am not telling him anything. I am just interpreting the events back to him. And it is high time he listened."

"But you didn't have to tell him right now. You know how miserable he is. You could have waited until things were better."

"There is no right time for these things, Sheila. Things would never be better if he continues this way."

Sheila blew her nose, but kept quiet.

"Your father is a selfish old man and now the laws of existence are bringing his avarice home to him. Who are you or I to stand in the way? He must suffer if he wants to stop being a jackal and become humane."

Suddenly Sheila broke in, quietly but decisively.

"Would you stop calling him a jackal? You may be a wise man and I might admire you for your wisdom, but you forget how long it has taken you to get where you are. And all the destruction that you have caused in the process."

She was right and I had nothing to say. For a long while neither of us spoke. Then Sheila spoke, her voice once again on the brink of tears.

"Don't you love him at all?"

The abruptness of her question surprised me.

"I suppose not."

I poured another cup of coffee.

I looked at my watch; it was getting late. I finished my coffee and got up. I walked over to the living room and Sheila came after me.

"It is very bright outside," I said, turning to Sheila. She was getting my shoes from under the divan and as I watched her arched back I was filled with a sense of sympathy for all Indian women who always had their back arched, stooping to someone's service.

"It is almost a year since I first came to your house," I said putting on my shoes.

She nodded dumbly like a child.

"What are you going to do?" Sheila said.

"I don't know exactly. I must get another job as soon as possible." She was silent for a while. Then she said,

"I wish you would stay here. It would be something to fall back upon."

"I am sorry, Sheila, I don't think I want to get involved with Mr. Khemka anymore. And, above all, he doesn't want me around, either. You will do much better without me."

Outside it was scorching hot. The roads were full of mirage and a hot wind blew through the empty streets, carrying clouds of dust before it. I stopped on the wayside and bought a packet of cigarettes from the wizened old lady who maintained a paan shop under a huge peepul tree. Then I went home and began to plan my search for a job.

18

FOR THE next two months I was away from Delhi, making the rounds at Calcutta and then Bombay, where the big corporations have their head offices. Each visit to one of these corporations consumed many days and I applied at only a few. It was difficult to get appointments with the appropriate people. When appointments came the interviews were perfunctory, superficial and poorly conducted.

I was disappointed but persistent. Finally, luck turned and I got offers from two companies in Bombay in the course of a week. The decision made, I returned to Delhi to pick up my things. It was a late Saturday afternoon when my train rolled into New Delhi station. The air was hot and humid. Summer had dissipated, overcome by its own intensity. The moisture-laden air presaged the monsoons under way. I threaded my way through the crowd of beggars and taxi drivers and thought to myself, "I'll miss the monsoons in Delhi."

My flat seemed almost as I'd left it, as if it was being preserved as a museum piece. My old servant had not understood the purpose of my wanderings but had remained at his post like a dutiful Casablanca. I explained to him that I was getting a job in Bombay and was leaving Delhi. He was dumbfounded, but tried to remain impassive.

"Why do you have to work in Bombay?" he asked.

"Mr. Khemka doesn't want me anymore."

"Have you done something wrong?"

I searched his face for a clue to his curiosity but his aged eyes only showed concern for me. "No, I have done nothing wrong, but he thinks I have, and he is the boss."

"But that is unfair," said the old man. "I don't think you can do anything wrong! He stressed the anything, and vehemently adjusted the belt of the white trousers I had had made for him. I noticed that the trousers were immaculate. What would he do when I was gone?

"Why don't you come with me to Bombay?" I suggested.

"I cannot do that," he said. "I grew up in this part of the country."

It sounded final, but I ventured that he likely would grow accustomed to Bombay after a while.

"I am too old to change, Sahib," he sighed resignedly. "In my youth I could have run around the world a dozen times, but now I am too old. In a year or two I have to start thinking of getting my daughters married."

He seemed to consider that task the irrefutable evidence of his helplessness. He sat beside me on the floor and rambled on about himself and his life. Fact and fiction and mythology were mixed queerly in his narrative. After some time I got up and started packing, but he kept talking.

Finally, he stopped talking and stood up, smoothing the wrinkles in his clean, white trousers.

"I must go and get some vegetables," he said. He looked brusque and efficient, but it was obvious from his eyes that he felt the presence of neither quality.

He started out and then paused. "I forgot to tell you, Sahib, Muthu came to see you a number of times while you were away. He seemed a little worried."

"Did he leave any message behind?"

184

"No, but he wanted to see you very badly."

"I'll see him," I said.

I went on about my packing and finished late in the evening, then went back to the station to reserve a seat for Bombay. It was off-season and plenty of seats were available. They booked me for the morning train on Monday.

Before I went to sleep that night I took a general stock of myself. In many ways the past had been a waste, but it had not been without its lessons. I had started adult life as a confused adolescent, engrossed with myself, searching for wisdom and the peace that comes with it. The journey had been long and tedious and still was not over.

And the future? In an ultimate sense, I knew, it would be as meaningless as the past. But, in a narrower sense, there would perhaps be useful tasks to be done; perhaps, if I were lucky, even a chance to redeem the past.

During the night the temperature suddenly dropped and by dawn it was raining. It was the first of the monsoons, carrying a freshness and coolness that was a welcome change from the humid heat of the previous day. I slept most of the day. When at last I decided to get out of bed it was almost four in the afternoon. A cool breeze pushed through the window but the sky was almost clear. I shaved and showered and had some tea. Then I went out to visit Muthu.

I had never been to Muthu's home but I knew the address. He lived near the western edge of the city where the government had constructed one room tenements for low-income groups. It was a dirty place laced with uncovered sewers that roared after the day's rain like miniature rivers beneath the earth. Wherever streets crossed, small hillocks of soggy trash stood as if no municipal truck had visited the place since the tenements were raised. Hordes of naked or semi-naked children squatted on the trash heaps and around them, emptying their bowels to the call of nature.

Muthu sat on a charpoy in front of his quarters. A bevy of children had crowded onto the charpoy with him but he seemed not to notice. He was lost in thought and did not see me until I stood directly in front of him. Then he rose suddenly, as if driven by a spring.

"Namaste, Sahib," he said, folding his hands.

"Namaste," I said.

There was a short silence and Muthu got nervous. He fidgeted and then turned to the children and told them to go and play somewhere else. But they simply moved more tightly together on the charpoy, making just enough room for me to sit down.

"When did you come?" Muthu asked.

"Yesterday," I said. "My servant told me you had come to visit me several times while I was away."

"Yes," Muthu said, and there was another awkward pause. But, as we talked, Muthu forgot himself and relaxed. We talked about the weather and how it sullied the streets instead of washing them clean. The children listened to our conversation for a while, then got bored and started their own small chatter.

"I didn't know you had so many children, Muthu," I said, for the number of small ones had surprised me.

"They are not all mine, sir. We all live here together."

"You mean you have some other family living with you?"

"My brother is staying with me right now; he does not have a job."

"But you have just one room?"

"Yes, we share it," Muthu said as if it was no trouble at all living with so many. "It is difficult at times, especially, in the mornings, but not so bad once you get used to it."

I'd heard much about overcrowding in Delhi, but this was the first time I had met somebody who lived with a dozen other people in the same room.

"It must be hard for you to have two families to support," I said, in an effort to communicate the sympathy I felt for him.

"It is not hard now because we are frugal, but it will be bad when I lose my job."

"Lose your job! Why?"

"I suppose I'll lose it," Muthu said. "Of course, you don't know about it. How could you, you have been away so long. It looks as if Mr. Khemka will lose control of his business. The Dasiya group is thinking of buying it over, and when that happens, most of us would naturally be asked to leave."

"I see," I said and waited for him to continue. But he sat silent, staring at his feet.

"Isn't Mr. Khemka looking after the business any more?" I asked.

"He is supposed to be, but we have not seen him for more than a month now."

186

"And Miss Khemka? Doesn't she come to the office?"

"She tried to manage things in the beginning. But I am afraid the business is rather beyond her." Muthu shifted uneasily on the bed and then added apologetically, "Of course that is only my opinion, sir."

"Of course. But what is the problem? Why are things breaking down so quickly?"

Muthu thought for a while. He rubbed the side of his nose as he always did when he was perplexed.

"Nobody seems to know, sir. Nobody seems to know what the matter is. Everybody seems so worried he can hardly do his own job, leave alone understanding what the problems are. Those who could get other jobs have already left. The rest of us spend the day wondering what we will do when the axe finally falls. Actually it is rather a pathetic situation."

Muthu looked about himself unseeing, as if he had suddenly found himself alone in unfamiliar surroundings.

"The problem is that we are all going to pieces," he said slowly. "There is no direction. We won't mind working twenty hours a day to keep ourselves in bread, but there is nobody around to tell us what to do. There have been almost no sales during the last month and the supply of money is getting choked off. To make matter worse, the creditors have got wind of Mr. Khemka's difficulties and they are clamouring for their money. As a matter of fact, two of them have already got their money back. It gets worse everyday. I'm sure sooner or later Mr Khemka would have to declare himself bankrupt. And then, some big banker like Mr. Dasiya would step in."

A girl of about eight came out of the house carrying two cups of tea. She moved slowly towards us, watching carefully to be sure the tea did not spill into the saucers. Her frock was dirty and too large for her. She shyly and carefully handed us the tea and then disappeared quickly into the house.

"That is my daughter, sir," Muthu said. "You must forgive my wife for not coming out herself. She is not well today."

"What's wrong?" I asked, concentrating on a crack in the side of the cup.

"She has tuberculosis and it gets rather bad in this weather."

"Oh, I am sorry." I said in surprise. "How long has she had it?"

"Almost ten years now," Muthu said. "But it is not so bad during winter."

We sipped our tea in silence, watching the dusk engulf the shabby scurvy slum in a black mist. So this was where Muthu came from every morning. This was the room where he spent his nights with eleven other people, one of them tubercular for ten years. Now some big banker was going to turn him out of that also, not because he did not want to work but because another big shot had made stupid mistakes and hadn't the guts to face up to them.

"What are you going to do, Muthu?"

"I don't know. Some years ago I could have gone back to our village. But now I can't. I sold my land to pay my father's debts. I shall try for a new job, but I don't have a degree and I am not sure whether somebody will give me a job. But things will work out."

"Are you frightened?"

"Yes," he replied briefly. After a while he continued, "Yes, I am very frightened. It is a great test. I wouldn't worry if these eleven people were not dependent on me. But it becomes difficult to remain calm when you find so many children going hungry most of the time."

Muthu had been trying to sound objective and cold, but his voice became thicker as he continued. Then, in a sudden burst of despair, he said.

"I wouldn't worry so much if I could at least be sure of food for these people, but right now, even that does not seem possible."

For a long while we were silent. Soon it became dark. Each house lit up, but the lights were dim and we could scarcely see each other's face. When Muthu finally spoke again he turned towards me but I could not see the expression on his face.

"All this is why I came to see you while you were away. I wanted to ask you to take over the office."

I had felt it coming and I knew he would say it. But I had no desire to get involved. I told him so.

"But it is not involvement, sir," he said. "Sometimes detachment lies in actually getting involved." He spoke quietly, but his voice was firm with conviction.

Again, for a long while we sat in the growing dark. I saw his point. Still, the old, nagging fear of getting involved with anything, anyone, was pushing through the mists of reason—a line of reasoning that led to the inevitable conclusion that for me, detachment consisted in getting involved with the world.

"So you want me to take over the office, do you, Muthu?"

"Yes, sir. You might save all of us."

"I don't want to, but I will give it a try, if you like."

"That is the most one can ask for, sir."

"And what if Mr. Khemka turned up and asked me to get out?"

"I don't think he will."

"I'll see you tomorrow then." I got up and stretched.

Muthu accompanied me to the taxi stand and saw me off. I went to the station and cashed in my ticket to Bombay, then went home. After dinner, much to the surprise of my servant, I unpacked my things and put them back as neatly as possible in their old places.

Word of my decision had already spread to the lowliest of Mr. Khemka's staff by the time I arrived at the office the next morning. Just to start off I called a meeting of the staff.

As I entered the room I had a strange sensation, something I had never before felt in life. I felt as if I had been dropped on a sinking ship and charged with the impossible task of taking it ashore. The men looked up at me unblinking, their expressionless faces reflecting neither love nor skepticism but only the accumulated despair of their weary lives. Until that moment I had not realised how considerably my visit to Muthu's home had affected me. If that was the sum total of Muthu's life, God alone knew what massive suffering lay behind those vacant eyes. It almost overwhelmed me.

I began quietly. I told them about my meeting with Muthu and why I was there. I said I was no great businessman. As a matter of fact, I said, I might turn out to be quite a poor one. I had no experience of this sort of thing before but I was willing to work with them if they all desired it.

I waited for their answer but none came. They continued to stare at me and presently the silence became oppressive. Perhaps they did not really want me.

"Do you want me," I repeated. Perhaps they sensed the touch of finality in may voice. The seniors, sitting in the front row, began to nod. Then one of them said,

"We have already discussed this among ourselves. We asked Muthu to request you—all of us." Now almost everyone was nodding.

189

"Very well, then," I said, unable to keep out a touch of emotion from my voice.

Silence hit the room again. Overhead the fans churned the hot, humid air. Sweat poured down my back in silent trickles.

After a while I continued.

"I know you are afraid the business will never recover, but things are not as bad as all that. After all, we were operating smoothly only a month ago. There is no reason why we cannot get this place on the right track again." The first objective, I told them, was to get organised and start working systematically. Then I asked if they had any questions. There was a long silence and then one of the clerks spoke up.

"Does this mean we will get all instructions from you from now on?"

"Yes."

"And what if we get directions from Miss Khemka or even Mr. Khemka?"

"You will not follow orders from either of them without first clearing them with me."

That seemed to settle any doubt. The meeting broke up and every body went back to work.

I spent the whole of the first day going through papers that had accumulated during the two months when no decisions were being made. It was a big pile of work and I had to stay at the office until late in the night. But the whole staff stayed with me. While we went along, the trouble spots became clear. Fortunately, my work with Mr. Khemka for one year had exposed me to nearly every problem. By ten o'clock we had identified a number of problems and laid plans for action.

As a first step towards cutting costs, I had the Khemka private offices dismantled to accommodate the marketing department that was being housed in another building. It was a big saving on rent.

For the next several weeks I worked late in the night. Most of the key staff members stayed at my side. I fell asleep as soon as I lay down. I woke up in the morning with just enough time to get to the office on time.

Those first few weeks were a life of strain. To make matters worse, fear of bankruptcy hung over us like a sword. One wrong step and we could have gone reeling down the road to dissolution. But, at the same time, I knew there was no choice for me except to remain

190

cool, as I had always been and to concentrate on decisive action. The fruit of it was really not my concern. By the end of the first month sales had begun to look up and the situation improved generally as a result.

One afternoon Sheila called on the telephone. It was the first word I'd had from her since I'd started working again. She was puzzled when I answered the call.

"Who is that?"

"Surrender Oberoi," I said.

"Oh, Sindi!" There was a pause, and then she hung up. I shrugged and burrowed back into my work.

An hour later Miss Khemka appeared at the office. Out of habit she headed straight for her private office. I was unable to restrain a smile when she finally noticed that the office was gone and she flushed in embarrassment.

"What happened to the cabins?"

"I had them dismantled," I said.

"But you can't do that!"

"It's done," I said.

She said nothing, but sat in a chair near my desk. She watched with keen interest while I discussed some papers. When I finally settled back in my chair and folded my hands behind my head and smiled at her, she asked.

"What is going on here?"

I told her what had happened, then gave her a brief review of what we had planned for the next few weeks. Among other things, I told her I was closing down the electric appliances division for the time being because it was draining too much capital and returns were nowhere near satisfactory. That division had been Mr. Khemka's pet project. Sheila objected vehemently.

"You can't do that!"

"Sheila, do you or do you not want me to run this place?" I asked her frankly.

She glanced at me and then averted her eyes. After a short pause she told me to do as I liked. Then she got up and said she was going. "If you can wait ten minutes I'll come with you," I said. "Maybe we could have tea at Wengers."

We occupied the same table at Wengers but it was a different union that met across the road. The speaker had already ascended the

E·16   63543

platform and the crowd was larger and more organised than the one
before. The wheels of industrialisation had moved substantially since
Sheila and I had last met.

"How's your father?" I asked.

"Haven't the office people told you?"

"I am told he has gone to pieces. Is that correct?"

"Yes," she said. There was a quaver in her voice.

"Is there hope for his acquittal?"

"No, I'm afraid. The government has a pretty strong case."

"Will he go to prison?"

"It looks like that," she said. "The trial is opening in two months."

"I'm sorry for you," I said.

We both looked out of the window. I had a feeling we were just
beginning to understand each other.

We watched the union activities across the road for a while and
then Sheila asked me how long I planned to stay with the company.

"I don't know," I said. "As long as I'm needed, I suppose."

"I didn't think you would come back."

"Nor did I."

"I thought you had become too detached to get involved in this
mess." A smile played at the corners of her mouth. I too smiled,
amused by the random absurdity of it all.

A waiter came along twirling his moustache, a dirty apron slung
across his shoulder. He stopped at our table and waited.

"Shall we have some tea?" Sheila said.

□ □ □